Coventry Patmore

Faithful for ever

Coventry Patmore

Faithful for ever

ISBN/EAN: 9783337414184

Printed in Europe, USA, Canada, Australia, Japan

Cover: Foto ©Andreas Hilbeck / pixelio.de

More available books at **www.hansebooks.com**

FAITHFUL FOR EVER.

BY

COVENTRY PATMORE,

AUTHOR OF "THE ANGEL IN THE HOUSE."

Of love that never found his earthly close,
What sequel?

TENNYSON.

BOSTON:
TICKNOR AND FIELDS.
M DCCC LXI.

BOOK I.

HONORIA.

-

FREDERICK GRAHAM TO HIS MOTHER.

MOTHER, I ſmile at your alarms!
 Againſt my Wiltſhire Couſins'
  charms
I 'm ſhielded by a prior ſpell.
The fever, love, as I 've heard tell,
Like other nurſery maladies,
Is never badly taken twice.
Have you forgotten Charlotte Hayes,
My playmate in the pleaſant days
At Knatchley, and her ſiſter, Anne;
The twins, ſo made on the ſame plan,
That one wore blue, the other white,

To mark them to their father's sight;
And how, at Knatchley harvesting,
You bade me kiss her in the ring,
Like Anne and all the others? You,
That never of my sickness knew,
Will laugh, yet had I the disease,
· And gravely, if the signs are these:

As, ere the Spring has any power,
The almond branch all turns to flower,
Though not a leaf is out, so she
The bloom of life provoked in me,
And, hard till then and selfish, I
Was thenceforth naught but sanctity
And service; life was mere delight
In being wholly good and right,
As she was; just, without a slur;
Honouring myself no less than her;
Obeying, in the loneliest place,
Ev'n to the slightest gesture, grace,
Assured that one so fair, so true,

Somehow he ſerved that was ſo too.
For me, hence weak towards the weak,
No more the unneſted blackbird's ſhriek
Startled the light-leaved wood; on high
Wander'd the gadding butterfly,
Unſcared by my flung cap; the bee,
Rifling the hollyhock in glee,
Was no more trapp'd with his own flower,
And for his honey ſlain.   Her power,
From great things even to the graſs
Through which the unfenced footways
     · paſs,
Was law, and that which keeps the law,
Cherubic gayety and awe ;
Day was her doing, ſo the lark
Had reaſon for his ſong ; the dark
In anagram innumerous ſpelt
Her name with ſtars that throbb'd and felt;
'T was the ſad ſummit of delight
To wake and weep for her at night;

She turn'd to triumph or to ſhame
The iſſue of each childiſh game;
The heart would come into my throat
At roſebuds; howſoe'er remote,
In oppoſition or conſent,
Each thing, or perſon, or event,
Or ſeeming neutral howſoe'er,
All, in the live, electric air,
Awoke, took aſpect, and confeſſ'd
In her a centre of unreſt,
Yea, ſtocks and ſtones within me bred
Anxieties of joy and dread.

  O, bright, apocalyptic ſky
O'erarching childhood! Far and nigh
Myſtery and obſcuration none,
Yet nowhere any moon or ſun!
What reaſon for theſe ſighs? What hope,
Daunting with its audacious ſcope
The diſconcerted heart, affects
Theſe ceremonies and reſpects?

Why ſtratagems in everything?
Why, why not kiſs her in the ring?
'T is nothing ſtrange that warriors bold,
Whoſe fierce, forecaſting eyes behold
The city they deſire to ſack,
Humbly begin their proud attack
By delving ditches two miles off,
Aware how the fair place would ſcoff
At haſty wooing ; but, O child,
Why thus approach thy playmate mild !
  One morning, when it fluſh'd my
        thought
That what in me ſuch wonder wrought
Was call'd, in men and women, love,
And, ſick with vanity thereof,
I, ſaying loud, " I love her," told
My ſecret to myſelf, behold
A criſis in my myſtery !
For, ſuddenly, I ſeem'd to be
Whirl'd round, and bound with ſhowers
    of threads,

As when the furious fpider fheds
Captivity upon the fly,
To ftill his buzzing till he die;
Only, with me, the bonds that flew,
Enfolding, thrill'd   me   through   and
        through
With blifs beyond aught heaven can have,
And pride to call myfelf her flave.

A long, green flip of wilder'd land,
With Knatchley Wood on either hand,
Sunder'd our home from hers. This day
Joy was mine as I went that way.
I stretch'd my arms to the fky, and fprang
O'er the elaftic fod, and fang
" I love her, love her!" to an air
Which with the words came, then and
        there ;
And even now, when I would know
All was not always dull and low,
I whiftle a turn of the fweet ftrain
Love taught me in that lonely lane.

Such glories fade, with no more mark
Than when the funfet turns to dark.
They die, the rapture and the grace .
Ineffable, nor leave a trace,
Except fometimes (fince joy is joy,
In fick or fane, in man or boy)
A heart which, having felt no lefs
Than pure and perfect happinefs,
Is duly dainty of delight ;
A patient, poignant appetite
For pleafures that exceed fo much
The poor things which the world calls
      fuch,
That, when thefe tempt it, then you may
The lion with a wifp of hay.
   That Charlotte, whom I fcarcely knew
From Anne but by her ribbons blue,
Was loved, Anne lefs than look'd at, fhows
That liking ftill by favour goes !
This Love is a divinity,

And holds his high election free
Of human merit; or, let's fay,
A child by ladies call'd to play,
But carelefs of their becks and wiles,
Till, feeing one who fits and fmiles
Like any elfe, yet only charms,
He cries to come into her arms.
Then, for my Coufins, fear me not!
None ever loved becaufe he ought.
Fatal were elfe this graceful house,
So full of light from ladies' brows.
There's Mary; Heaven in her appears
Like funfhine through the fhower's laft
        tears;
Mildred's of Earth, but gayer far
Than moft men's thoughts of Heaven are;
But, for Honoria, Heaven and Earth
Seal'd amity in her fweet birth.
The noble Girl! With whom she talks
She knights firft with her fmile; fhe walks,

Stands, dances, to fuch fweet effect
Alone fhe feems to go erect.
The brighteft and the chafteft brow ·
Rules o'er a cheek which feems to fhow
That love, as a mere vague fufpenfe
Of apprehenfive innocence,
Perturbs her heart ; love without aim
Or object, like the holy flame
That in the Veftals' Temple glow'd,
Without the image of a god.
And this fimplicity moft pure
She fets off with no lefs a lure
Of culture, nobly fkill'd to raife
The power, the pride, and mutual praife
Of human perfonality
Above the common fort fo high
It makes fuch homely fouls as mine
Wonder how brightly life may fhine.
Ah, how you 'd love her ! Even in drefs
She makes the common mode exprefs.

New knowledge of what's fit fo well
'T is virtue gayly vifible!
Nay, but her filken fafh to me
Were more than all morality,
But that the old, fweet, feverous ill
Has left me mafter of my will.

II.

MRS. GRAHAM TO FREDERICK.

2

MRS. GRAHAM TO FREDERICK.

MY deareſt Child, Honoria ſways
    A double power, through Char-
       lotte Hayes!
In minds to firſt-love's memory pledged
The ſecond Cupid's born full-fledged.
The Churchills came, laſt Spring, to Spa,
And ſtay'd with me a week. I ſaw,
And own I trembled for the day
When you ſhould ſee that beauty, gay
And pure as apple-blooms, that ſhow
Outſide a bluſh and inſide ſnow;
That high and touching elegance
Which even your raptures ſcarce enhance.

Ah, hafte from her enchanting fide !
No friend for you, far lefs a bride.
But, warning from a hope fo wild,
I wrong you.   Yet this know, my child:
He that but lends his heart to hear
The mufic of a foreign fphere,
Is thenceforth lonely, and for all
His days like one who treads the Wall
Of China, and on this hand fees
Cities and their civilities,
And on the other lions.   Well,
(Your rafh reply I thus foretell,)
Good is the knowledge of what's fair,
Though bought with temporal defpair.
Yes, good for one, but not for two !
Will it content your wife that you
Should pine for love, in love's embrace,
Becaufe you've known a prouder grace;
Difturb with inward fighs your reft,
Becaufe, though good, fhe's not the beft;

Her acts of fondnefs almoft fhun,

Becaufe they are handfomer meant than
　　　done ?

You would, you think, be juft and kind,

And keep your counfel !　You will find

You cannot fuch a fecret keep.

'T will out, like murder, in your fleep ;

A touch will tell it, though, for pride,

She may her bitter knowledge hide ;

And, whilft fhe accepts love's make-
　　　believe,

You 'll twice defpife what you 'd deceive.

　For your fake I am glad to hear

You fail fo foon.　I fend you, dear,

A trifling prefent ; 't will fupply

Your Salifbury cofts.　You have to buy

Almoft an outfit for this cruife !

But many are good enough to ufe

Again, among the things you fend

To give away.　My maid fhall mend

And let you have them back.   Adieu !
Tell me of all you are and do.
I know, thank God, whate'er it be,
'T will need no veil 'twixt you and me.

III.

FREDERICK TO HIS MOTHER.

FREDERICK TO HIS MOTHER.

THE multitude of voices blythe
    Of early day, the hiffing fcythe
Athwart the dew drawn and withdrawn,
The noify peacock on the lawn,
Thefe, and the fun's eye-gladding gleam,
This morning, chafed the fweeteft dream
That e'er fhed penitential grace
On life's forgetful commonplace ;
Yet 't was no fweeter than the fpell
To which I woke to fay farewell.

    Noon finds me ninety miles removed
From her who muft not be beloved ;
And us the whole fea foon fhall part,

Heaving for aye without a heart!
But why, dear mother, warn me fo?
I love Mifs Churchill? Ah, no, no!
I view, enchanted, from afar,
And love her as I love a ftar.
For, not to fpeak of colder fear,
Which keeps my fancy calm, I hear,
Under her life's gay progrefs hurl'd,
The wheels of the preponderant world,
Set fharp with fwords that fool to flay
Who blunders from a poor byway,
To covet beauty with a crown
Of earthly blefling added on;
And fhe's fo much, it feems to me,
Beyond all women womanly,
I dread to think how he fhould fare
Who came fo near as to defpair.

No more of this! Dear mother, pleafe
To fend my books to Plymouth. Thefe,
When I go hence, fhall turn all hours

To profit, and amend my powers.
I've time on board to fill my poſt,
And yet make up for ſchooling loſt
Through young ſea-ſervice.   They all
        ſpeak
German and French; and theſe, with
        Greek,
Which Doctor Churchill thought I knew,
And Hiſtory, which I'm ill in too,
Will ſtop a gap I ſomewhat dread,.
After the happy life I've led
Among my couſins; and 't will be
To abridge the ſpace from them to me.
    Yonder the ſullen veſſel rides
Where my obſcure condition hides.
Waves ſcud to ſhore againſt the wind,
That flings the ſprinkling ſurf behind;
In port the bickering pennons ſhow
Which way the ſhips would gladly go;
Through Edgecumbe Park the rooted trees

Are toffing, recklefs, in the breeze;
On top of Edgecumbe's firm-fet tower,
As foils, not foibles, of its power,
The light vanes do themfelves adjuft
To every veering of the guft :
By me alone may naught be given
To guidance of the airs of heaven ?
In battle or peace, in calm or ftorm,
Should I my daily tafk perform,
(Better a thoufand times for love,)
Who fhould my fecret foul reprove !

 Mother, I 've ftriven to conceal,
Yes, from myfelf, how much I feel ;
In vain. With tears my fight is dull,
My coufin makes my heart fo full.
Her happy beauty makes a man
Long to lay down his life ! How can
Aught to itfelf feem thus enough,
When I have fo much need thereof !
Bleft is her place ! blifsful is fhe ;

And I, departing, feem to be
Like the ftrange waif that comes to run ˌ
A few days flaming near the fun,
And carries back, through boundlefs night,
Its leffening memory of light.
O, my dear mother ! I confefs ˏ
To a weak grief of homeleffnefs,
Unfelt, fave once, before.   'T is years
Since fuch a fhower of girlifh tears
Difgraced me !   But this wretched Inn,
At Plymouth, is fo full of din,
Talkings and trampings to and fro.
And then my fhip, to which I go
To-night, is no more home.   I dread,
As ftrange, the life I long have led ;
And as, when firft I went to fchool,
And found the horror of a rule,
Which only afk'd to be obey'd,
I lay and wept, of dawn afraid,
And thought, with burfting heart, of one

Who, from her little, wayward ſon,
Required obedience, but above
Obedience ſtill regarded love,
So change I that enchanting place,
The abode of innocence and grace
And gayety without reproof,
For the black gun-deck's lowering roof,
Blind and inevitable law,
Which makes light duties burdens, awe
Which is not reverence, laughters gain'd
At coſt of purities profaned,
And whatſoever moſt may ſtir
Remorſeful paſſion towards her,
Whom to behold is to depart
From all defect of life and heart.
　By her inſtructed what may be
Ƭhe joy of true ſociety,
Frightful is ſolitude; yet 't is,
Compared with ſuch infeſtment, bliſs.
　But, mother, I shall go on shore,

And fee my Coufin yet once more !
'T were wild to hope for her, you fay ?
I've torn and caft thofe words away.
Surely there's hope !   For life 't is well
Love without hope's impoffible ;
So, if I love, it is that hope
Is not outfide the outer fcope
Of fancy.   You fpeak truth : this hour,
I muft refift, or lofe the power.
What ! and, when fome short months are
        o'er,
Be not much other than before ?
Decline the high, harmonious fphere
In which I'm held, but while fhe's dear ?
In unrefpective peace forget
Thofe eyes for which my own are wet
With that delicious, fruitful dew
Which, check'd, will never flow anew ?
For daily life's dull, fenfelefs mood,
Slay the fharp nerves of gratitude

And fweet allegiance, which I owe,
Whether she cares for me or no ?
Nay, Mother, I, forewarn'd, prefer
To want for all in wanting her.

   For all ?   Love's beft is not bereft
Ever from him to whom is left
The truft that God will not deceive
His creature, fafhion'd to believe
The prophecies of pure defire.
Not lofs, not death, my love shall tire.
A myftery does my heart foretell ;
Nor do I prefs the oracle
For explanations.   Leave me alone,
And let in me love's will be done.

IV.

FREDERICK TO HIS MOTHER.

3

FREDERICK TO HIS MOTHER.

FASHION'D by Heaven and by art
   So is fhe, that fhe makes the heart
Ache and o'erflow with tears, that grace
So wonderful fhould have for place
The unworthy earth! To fee her fmile,
As ignorant of her hap the while,
And walk this howling wafte of fin,
As only knowing the heaven within,
Is fweet, and does for pity ftir
Paffion to be her minifter;
Wherefore laft night I lay awake,
And faid, "Ah, Lord! for thy love's fake,
Give not this darling child of thine

To care lefs reverent than mine!"
And, as true faith was in my word,
I truft, I truft that I was heard.

    The waves, this morning, fped to land,
And fhouted hoarfe to touch the ftrand,
Where Spring, that goes not out to fea,
Lay laughing in her lovely glee;
And, fo, my life was funlit fpray
And tumult, as, once more to-day,
For long farewell did I draw near
My Coufin defperately dear.
Faint, fierce, the truth that hope was
          none
Gleam'd like the lightning in the fun;
Yet, hope I had, and joy thereof!
The father of love is hope, (though love
Lives orphan'd on, when hope is dead,)
And, out of my immediate dread
And crifis of the coming hour,
Did hope itfelf draw fudden power.

So the hot-brooding ſtorm, in Spring,
Makes all the birds begin to ſing.

 Mother, your foreſight did not err :
I've loſt the world, and not won her.
And yet, ah, laugh not, when you think
What cup of life I ſought to drink !
The bold, ſaid I, have climb'd to bliſs
Abſurd, impoſſible, as this,
With naught to help them but ſo great
A heart it faſcinates their fate.
If ever Heaven back'd man's deſire,
Mine, being ſmirchleſs altar-fire,
Muſt come to paſs, and it will be
That ſhe will wait, when ſhe ſhall ſee,
This evening, how I go to get
By means unknown I know not yet
Quite what, but ground whereon to ſtand,
And plead more plainly for her hand !

 While thus I raved, and caſt in hope
A ſuperſtitious horoſcope,

I reach'd the Dean's. The woman faid,
"Mifs Churchill's out." "Had fhe been
     dead,"
I cried, "'t were much the fame to me,
Who go, this very night, to fea."
"Nay, fir, fhe's only gone to prayer;
And here fhe comes, acrofs the Square."
(O, but to be the unbanifhed fod
She daily treads, all bright from God!)
    And now, though fomething in her face
Portended "No!" with fuch a grace
It burthen'd me with thankfulnefs,
Nothing was credible but "Yes!"
Therefore, through time's clofe preffure
     bold,
I praifed myfelf, and boaftful told
My deeds at Acre, ftrained the chance
I had of honour and advance
In war to come; and would not fee
Sad filence meant "What's this to me!"

When half my precious hour was gone,
She rofe to greet a Mr. Vaughan;
And, as the image of the moon
Breaks up, within fome ftill lagoon
That feels the foft wind fuddenly,
Or tide frefh flowing from the fea,
And turns to giddy flames that go
Over the water to and fro,
Thus, when he took her hand to-night,
Her lovely gravity of light
Was fcattered into many fmiles
And flattering weaknefs. Hope beguiles
No more my heart, dear Mother. He,
By jealous looks, o'erhonour'd me!
  With naught to do, and fondly fain
To hear her finging once again,
I ftay'd, and turn'd her mufic o'er;
Then came fhe with me to the door.
"Deareft Honoria," I faid,
(By my defpair familiar made,)

"Heaven blefs you!"   O, to have back
    then ftepp'd,
And fall'n upon her neck, and wept,
And faid, "My friend, I owe you all
I am, and have, and hope for.   Call
For fome poor fervice; let me prove
To you, or him here whom you love,
My duty.   Any folemn tafk,
For life's whole courfe, is all I afk!"
Then fhe muft furely have wept too,
And faid, "My friend, what can you
    do?"
And I fhould have replied, "I'll pray
For you and him three times a day,
And, all day, morning, noon, and night,
My life fhall be fo high and right
That never Saint yet fcaled the ftairs
Of heaven with more availing prayers!"
But this, (and, as good God fhall blefs
Somehow my end, I'll do no less,)

I had no right to fpeak.   Oh, fhame,
So rich a love, fo poor a claim!
   My Mother, now my only friend,   .
Farewell.   The fchool-books which you
      fend
I fhall not want, and fo return.
Give them away, or fell, or burn.
Addrefs to Malta.   Would I might
But be your little Child to-night,
And feel your arms about me fold,
Againft this lonelinefs and cold!

V.

MRS. GRAHAM TO FREDERICK.

'

MRS. GRAHAM TO FREDERICK.

MY own dear Child, Honoria's choice
     Shows what fhe is, and I rejoice
You did not win her.   Felix Vaughan
Preferr'd to you ?   My faith is gone
In her fine fenfe !   And, thus, you fee
You were too good for her !   Ah, me,
The folly of thefe girls : they doff
Their pride to fleek fuccefs, and fcoff
At far more noble fire and might
That woo them from the duft of fight !
    But now, Dear, fince the ftorm is paft,
Your fky fhould not remain o'ercaft.
A fea life's dull, and, fo, beware

Of nourishing, for zest, despair.
Remember, Frederick, this makes twice
You've been in love; then why not thrice,
Or ten times?   But a wise man shuns
To say "All's over" more than once.
Religion, duty, books, work, friends,
Are anodynes, if not amends.
I'll not urge that a young man's soul
Is scarce the measure of the whole
Earthly and heavenly universe,
To which he inveterately prefers
The one beloved woman.   Best
Speak to the senses' interest,
Which brooks no mystery nor delay:
Frankly reflect, my Son, and say,
Was there no secret hour, of those
Pass'd at her side in Sarum Close,
When, to your spirit's sick alarm,
It seem'd that all her marvellous charm
Was marvellously fled?   The cause

'T is like you fought not.   This it was:
It happen'd, for that hour, her grace
Of voice, adornment, pofture, face
Was what already heart and eye
Had ponder'd to fatiety ;
And fo the good of life was o'er,
Until fome laugh not heard before,
Some novel fafhion in her hair,
Or ftyle of putting back her chair,
Reftored the heavens.   Gather thence
The lofs-confoling inference !

   I blame not beauty.   It beguiles,
With lovely motions and fweet fmiles,
Which while they pleafe us pafs away,
The fpirit to lofty thoughts that ftay,
And lift the whole of after-life,
Unlefs you take the thing to wife,
Which then feems naught, or ferves to
     flake
Defire, as when a lovely lake

Far off fcarce fills the exulting eye
Of one athirft, who comes thereby,
And inappreciably fips
The deep, with difappointed lips.
To fail is forrow, yet confefs
That love pays dearly for fuccefs !
I blame not beauty, but complain
Of the heart, which can fo ill fuftain
Delight.   Our griefs declare our Fall,
But how much more our joys ! They pall
With plucking, and celeftial mirth
Can find no footing on the earth,
More than the bird of paradife,
Which only lives the while it flies.
　　Think, alfo, how 't would fuit your
　　　　pride
To have this woman for a bride.
Whate'er her faults, fhe's one of thofe
To whom the world's laft polifh owes
A further grace, which all who afpire

To courtlieſt cuſtom muſt acquire.
The world's her duty and her ſphere;
But you have ſtill been lonely, Dear.
(Oh, law perverſe, that lonelineſs
Breeds love, ſociety ſucceſs!)
Though young, 'twere now o'er late in
      life
To train yourſelf for ſuch a wife;
So ſhe would fit herſelf to you,
As women, when they marry, do.
For, ſince 'tis for their dignity
Their lords ſhould ſit like lords on high,
They willingly deteriorate
To a ſtep below their rulers' ſtate;
And 'tis the commoneſt of things
To ſee an angel, gay with wings,
Lean weakly on a mortal's arm!
Honoria would put off the charm
Of cultured grace that caught your love,
For fear you ſhould not ſeem above

Herſelf in faſhion and degree,
As in true merit.   Thus, you ſee,
'T were little kindneſs, wiſdom none,
To light your barn with ſuch a ſun.

VI.

FREDERICK TO HIS MOTHER.

FREDERICK TO HIS MOTHER.

DEAR Mother, do not write her name
    With the leaſt word or hint of blame.
Who elſe ſhall diſcommend her choice,
I giving it my hearty voice?
She marry me?   I loved too well
To think it good or poſſible.
Ah, never near her beauties come
The buſineſs of the narrow home!
Far fly from her dear face, that ſhows
The funſhine lovelier than the roſe,
The ſordid gravity they wear
Who poverty's baſe burthen bear!
(And they are poor who come to miſs

Their cuftom, though a crown be this.)
My hope was, that the wheels of fate,
For my exceeding need, might wait,
And fhe, unfeen amidft all eyes,
Move fightlefs, till I fought the prize,
With honour, in an equal field.
But then came Vaughan, to whom I yield
With grace as much as any man,
In such caufe, to another can.
Had fhe been mine, it feems to me
That I had that integrity
And only joy in her delight —
But each is his own favourite
In love !   The thought to bring me reft
Is that of us fhe takes the beft.

    'T was but to fee him to be fure
That choice for her remain'd no more !
His brow, fo gayly clear of craft;
His wit, the timely truth that laugh'd
To find itfelf fo well exprefs'd ;

His words, abundant yet the best ;
His fpirit, of fuch handfome fhow
You faw not that his looks were fo ;
His bearing, profpects, birth, all thefe
Might well, with fmall fuit, greatly pleafe ;
How greatly, when fhe faw arife
The reflex fweetnefs of her eyes
In his, and every breath defer
Humbly its bated life to her ;
Whilft power and kindnefs of command,
Which women can no more withftand
Than we their grace, were ftill unquell'd,
And force and flattery both compell'd
Her foftnefs ! . Say I'm worthy.   I
Grew, in her prefence, cold and fhy.
It awed me, as an angel's might
In raiment of reproachful light.
Her gay looks told my fombre mood
That what's not happy is not good ;
And, juft becaufe 't was life to pleafe,

Death to repel her, truth and eafe
Deferted me ; I ftrove to talk,
And ftammered foolifhnefs ; my walk
Was like a drunkard's ; once fhe took
My arm ; it ftiffen'd, ached, and fhook ;
I guefs'd her thought, and could have
          dropp'd ;
The ftreams of life within me ftopp'd.
A likely wooer !   Blame her not ;
Nor ever fay, dear Mother, aught
Againft that perfectnefs which is
My ftrength, as once it was my blifs.
    Nor let us chafe at focial rules.
Leave that to poets and to fools.
Clay graffs and clods conceive the rofe,
So bafe ftill fathers beft.   Life owes
Itfelf to bread ; enough thereof
And eafy days condition love ;
And, highly train'd, love's rofes thrive,
No more pale, fcentlefs petals five,

Which moiften the confiderate eye
To fee what hafte they make to die,
But heavens of brightnefs and perfume,
Which, month by month, renew the bloom
Of art-born graces, when the year
In all the natural grove is fere.

　　Thank God, I partly can defcry
The meaning of humanity !
In fight of him who fees it float
As many an ifolated mote
In accidental light or dark,
And wants the inftructed fenfe to mark
Its method, and the ear to hear
The moving mufic of its fphere,
What wonder if his private lofs
Seems an intolerable crofs,
Not to be fuffer'd, in mere awe
Of what he calls the world's cold law ?
But he who once, with joy of foul,
Has had the vifion of the whole,

Though to the wringing of his heart,
Will never more prefer the part.
Blame none, then! Bright let be the air
About my lonely cloud of care.
  "Religion, duty, books, work, friends:"
'T is good advice, but there it ends.
I'm fick for what they have not got.
Send no more books; they help me not.
I'm hurt, and find no falve for that
In gofpels of the cricket-bat
Or anvil; and, for zoophytes,
And algæ, and Italian rights,
Myfelf and every foul I fee
Are nearer, dearer myftery,
And fubject to my proper will,
To fome extent, for good or ill.
And, as for work, Mother, I find
The life of man is in his mind,
(Though, truft the ftrains the fafhion
    ftrums,

It feems 't is rather in his thumbs !)
To work is well, nay, labour is,
They fay, the bread of fouls.   If 't is,
We do not worfhip corn and yeaft ;
Indeed, they fcarcely make a feaft !
Bread's needful, but the rule ftands fo
That needful moft is oft moft low.
I act my calling, yet there's ftill
A void which duty cannot fill.
What though the inaugural hour of right
Comes ever with a keen delight !
Little relieves the labour's heat,
Or crowns the labour when complete ;
And life, in fact, is not lefs dull
For being very dutiful.
" The ftately homes of England," lo,
" How beautiful they ftand ! "   They owe
How much to me and fuch as me
Their beauty of fecurity !
But who can long a low work mend

By looking to a lofty end ?
And let me, fince 't is truth, confefs
The want's not filled by godlinefs.
God is a tower without a ftair,
And His perfection love's defpair.
'T is he fhall judge me when I die;
He fuckles with the hiffing fly
The fpider; gazes patient down,
Whilft rapine grips the helplefs town.
His vaft love holds all this and more.
In confternation I adore !
Nor can I eafe this aching gulf
With friends, the pictures of myfelf.

  Then marvel not that I recur
From each and all of thefe to her.
For more of heaven than her have I
No fenfitive capacity.
Had I but her, ah, what the gain
Of owning aught but that domain !
Nay, heaven's extent, however much,

Cannot be more than many fuch ;
And, fhe being mine, fhould God to me
Say, "Lo! my Child, I give to thee
All heaven befides," what could I then,
But, as a child, to Him complain
That, whereas my dear Father gave
A little fpace for me to have
In his great garden, now, o'erbleft,
I've that, indeed, but all the reft,
Which, fomehow, makes it feem I've got
All but my only cared-for plot.
Enough was that for my weak hand
To tend, my heart to underftand.

 Oh, the fick thought, 'twixt her and me
There's nothing, and the weary fea !

VII.

FREDERICK TO HIS MOTHER.

FREDERICK TO HIS MOTHER.

MOTHER, in fcarcely two hours more
    I fet my foot on Englifh fhore,
Two years untrod! and, ftrange to tell,
Nigh miff'd, through laft night's ftorm.
        There fell
A man from the fhrouds, that roar'd to
        quench
Even the billows' blaft and drench.
None elfe but me was by to mark
His loud cry in the louder dark,
Dark, fave when lightning fhow'd the
        deeps
Standing about in ftony heaps.

5

No time for choice !   A fortunate flafh
Flamed as he rofe ; a dizzy fplafh,
A ftrange, inopportune delight
Of mounting with the billowy might,
And falling, with a thrill again
Of pleafure fhot from feet to brain,
And both paced deck, ere any knew
Our peril.   Round us prefs'd the crew.
" Your duty was to let him drown,"
The Captain faid, and feign'd a frown ;
But wonder fill'd the eyes of moft.
As if the man who had loved and loft
Honoria dared no more than that !

    My days have elfe been ftale and flat.
This life's, at beft, if juftly fcann'd,
A tedious walk by the other's ftrand,
With, here and there caft up, a piece
Of coral or of ambergris,
Which boafted of abroad, we ignore
The burthen of the barren fhore.

Often might I my letters fill
With how the nerves refufe to thrill;
How, throughout doubly-darken'd days,
I cannot recollect her face;
How to my heart her name to tell
Is beating on a broken bell;
And, to fill up the abhorrent gulf,
Scarce loving her, I hate myfelf.

    Yet, latterly, with ftrange delight,
Rich tides have rifen in the night,
And fweet dreams chafed the fancies denfe
Of waking life's dull fomnolence.
I fee her as I knew her, grace
Already glory in her face;
I move about, I cannot reft,
For the proud brain and joyful breaft
I have of her. Or elfe I float
The pilot of an idle boat,
Alone with fun, and fky, and fea,
And her, the fourth fimplicity.

Or Mildred, to fome queftion, cries,
(Her merry mifchief in her eyes,)
" The Ball, oh, Frederick will go;
Honoria will be there!" and, lo,
As moifture fweet my feeing blurs
To hear my name fo link'd with hers,
A mirror joins, by guilty chance,
Either's averted, watchful glance!
Or with me, in the Ball-Room's blaze,
Her brilliant mildnefs thrids the maze;
Our thoughts are lovely, and each word
Is mufic in the mufic heard,
And all things feem but parts to be
Of one perfiftent harmony,
By which I'm made divinely bold;
The fecret, which fhe knows, is told;
And, laughing with a lofty blifs
Of innocent accord, we kifs;
About her neck my pleafure weeps;
Againft my lip the filk vein leaps;

Then fays an Angel, " Day or night,
If yours you feek, not her delight,
Although by fome ftrange witchery
It feems you kifs her, 't is not fhe.;
But whilft you languifh at the fide
Of a fair-foul phantafmal bride,
Surely a dragon and ftrong tower
Guard the true lady in her bower."
And I fay, " Dear my Lord, Amen ! "
And the true lady kifs again.
Or elfe fome wafteful malady
Devours her fhape and dims her eye;
No charms are left, where all were rife,
Except her voice, which is her life,
Wherewith fhe, for her foolifh fear,
Says trembling, " Do you love me, Dear ? "
And I reply, "Ah, Sweet, I vow
I never loved but half till now."
She turns her face to the wall at this,
And fays, " Go, Love, 't is too much blifs."

And then a fudden pulfe is fent
About the founding firmament
In fmitings as of filver bars;
The bright diforder of the ftars
Is folved by mufic; far and near,
Through infinite diftinctions clear,
Their two-fold voices' deeper tone
Thunders the Name which all things
        own,
And each ecftatic treble dwells
On one whereof none other tells;
And we, fublimed to fong and fire,
Take order in the wheeling quire,
Till from the throbbing fphere I ftart,
Waked by the beating of my heart.
    Such dreams as thefe come night by
        night,
Difturbing day with their delight.
Portend they nothing?   Who can tell!
God yet may do fome miracle.

'T is now two years, and fhe's not wed,
Or you would know! He may be dead, '
Or mad and wooing fome one elfe,
And fhe, much moved that nothing quells
My conftancy, or, merely wroth
With fuch a wretch, accept my troth
To fpite him; or her beauty's gone,
(And that's my dream!) and this vile
   Vaughan
Takes her releafe; or tongues malign,
Convincing all men's ears but mine,
Have fmirch'd her: ah, 't would move
   her, fure,
To find I only worfhipp'd more!
Nay, now I think, haply amifs
I read her words and looks, and his,
That night! Did not his jealoufy
Show — Good my God, and can it be
That I, a modeft fool, all bleft,
Nothing of fuch a heaven guefs'd?

Oh, chance too frail, yet frantic fweet.
To-morrow fees me at her feet!

 Yonder, at laft, the glad fea roars
Along the facred Englifh fhores!
There lies the lovely land I know,
Where men and women lordlieft grow;
There peep the roofs where more than
  kings
Poftpone ftate cares to country things,
And many a gay queen fimply tends
The babes on whom the world depends;
There curls the wanton cottage fmoke
Of him that drives but bears no yoke;
There laughs the realm where low and
  high
Are lieges to fociety,
And life has all too wide a fcope,
Too free a profpect for its hope,
For any private good or ill,
Except difhonour, quite to fill!

Poſtscript. Since this was penn'd, I read
That "Mr. Vaughan, on Tueſday, wed ,
The beautiful Miſs Churchill." So
That's over; and to-morrow I go
To take up my new poſt on board
The Wolf, my peace at laſt reſtored,
For all the ſhowering tears that ſoak
This paper. Grief is now the cloak
I fold about me to prevent
The deadly chill of a content
With any near or diſtant good,
Except the exact beatitude
Which love has ſhown to my deſire.
You'll point to "other joys and higher."
I hate and diſavow all bliſs
As none for me which is not this.
Think not I blaſphemouſly cope
With God's decrees, and caſt off hope.
How, when, and where can mine ſucceed?
I'll truſt He knows who made my need!

VIII.

FREDERICK TO HIS MOTHER.

FREDERICK TO HIS MOTHER.

I THOUGHT the worſt had brought
    me balm,
'T was but the tempeſt's central calm.
Vague ſinkings of the heart aver
That dreadful wrong has come to her,
And o'er this whim I brood and doat,
And learn its agonies by rote.
As if I loved it, early and late
I make familiar with my fate,
And feed, with faſcinated will,
On very dregs of finiſh'd ill.
I think, ſhe's near him now, alone,
With wardſhip and protection none ;

Alone, perhaps, in the hindering ſtreſs
Of airs that claſp him with her dreſs,
They wander whiſpering by the wave ;
And haply now, in ſome ſea-cave
Where the ſalt ſand is rarely trod,
They laugh, they kiſs. O God! O God!
   Baſeneſs of men !   Purſuit being o'er,
Doubtleſs the Lover feels no more
The awful heaven of ſuch a Bride,
But, lounging, let's her pleaſe his pride
With fondneſs, guerdons her careſs
With little names, and twiſts a treſs
Round idle fingers.   If 't is ſo,
Why then I'm happier of the two !
Better, for lofty loſs, like pain,
Than low content with lofty gain.
Poor, fooliſh Dove, to truſt from me
Her happineſs and dignity !
   Thus, all day long till frightful night
I fear ſhe's harm'd by his delight,

And when I lay me down at even
'T is Hades lit with neighbouring Heaven.
There comes a fmile acutely fweet
Out of the picturing dark ; I meet
The ancient franknefs of her gaze,
That fimple, bold, and living blaze
Of great good-will and innocence,
And perfect joy proceeding thence !
Ah ! made for Earth's delight, yet fuch
The mid-fea air's too grofs to touch.
At thought of which, the foul in me
Is as the bird that bites a bee,
And darts abroad on frantic wing,
Tafting the honey and the fting ;
And, moaning where all round me fleep
Amidft the moaning-of the deep,
I ftart at midnight from my bed —
And have no right to ftrike him dead.
  What world is this that I am in,
Where chance turns fanctity to fin !

'T is crime henceforward to defire
The only good, the facred fire
Of all the univerfe is hell !
I hear a Voice that argues well :
"The Heaven hard has fcorn'd your cry ;
Fall down and worfhip me, and I
Will give you peace ; go and profane
This pangful love, fo pure, fo vain,
And thereby win forgetfulnefs
And pardon of the fpirit's excefs,
Which foar'd too nigh that jealous Heaven
Ever, fave thus, to be forgiven.
No Gofpel has come down that cures
With better gain a lofs like yours.
Be pious ! Give the beggar pelf,
And love your neighbour as yourfelf !
You, who yet love, though all is o'er,
And fhe'll ne'er be your neighbour more,
With foul which can in pity fmile
That aught with fuch a meafure vile

As felf fhould be at all named 'love!'
Your fanctity the priefts reprove,
Your cafe of grief they wholly mifs.
The Man of Sorrows names not this!
'The years,' they fay, 'graft love divine
On the lopp'd ftock of love like thine,
The wild tree dies not, but converts.'
So be it; but the lopping hurts,
The graff takes tardily! Men ftanch
Meantime with earth the bleeding branch.
There's nothing heals one woman's lofs,
And lightens life's eternal crofs
With intermiffion of found reft,
Like lying in another's breaft.
The cure is, to your thinking, low!
Is not life all, henceforward, fo?"

Ill Voice, at leaft thou calm'ft my mood;
I'll fleep! But, as I thus conclude,
The intrufions of her grace difpel
The comfortable glooms of hell.

6

A wonder! Ere thefe lines were dried,
Vaughan and my Love, his three-days'
      Bride,
Became my guefts.   I look'd, and, lo!
In beauty foft as is the fnow
And powerful as the avalanche,
She lit the deck. The Heav'n-fent chance!
She fmiled, furprifed.   They came to
      fee
The fhip, not thinking to meet me.
At infinite diftance fhe's my day!
What then to him?   Howbeit they fay
'T is not fo funny in the fun
But men might live cool lives thereon!
  All's well; for I have feen arife
That reflex fweetnefs of her eyes
In his, and watch'd his breath defer
Humbly its bated life to her,
His *wife*.   Dear Love, fhe's fafe in his
Devotion; and the thought of this,

Though more than ever I admire,
Removes her out of my defire.
   They bade adieu ; I faw them go
Acrofs the fea ; and now I know
The ultimate hope I refted on,
The hope beyond the grave, is gone,
The hope that, in the heavens high,
At laft it fhould appear that I
Loved moft, and fo, by claim divine,
Should have her, in the heavens, for mine,
According to fuch nuptial fort
As may fubfift in the holy court,
Where, if there are all kinds of joys
To exhauft the multitude of choice
In many manfions, then there are
Loves perfonal and particular,
Confpicuous in the glorious fky
Of univerfal charity,
As Hefper in the funrife.   Now
I 've feen them, I believe their vow

Immortal; and the dreadful thought,·
That he leſs honour'd than he ought
Her ſanctity, is laid to reſt,
And, bleſſing them, I too am bleſt.
My good-will, as a ſpringing air,
Unclouds a beauty in deſpair;
I ſtand beneath the ſky's pure cope
Unburthen'd even by a hope;
And peace unſpeakable, a joy
Which hope would deaden and deſtroy,
Like ſunſhine fills the airy gulf
Left by the vaniſhing of ſelf.
That I have known her; that ſhe moves
Somewhere all-graceful; that ſhe loves,
And is belov'd, and that ſhe's ſo
Moſt happy; and to heaven will go,
Where I may meet with her, (yet this
I count but adventitious bliſs,)
And that the full, celeſtial weal
Of all ſhall ſenſitively feel

The partnerſhip and work of each,
And, thus, my love and labour reach
Her region, there the more to bleſs
Her laſt, conſummate happineſs,
Is guerdon up to the degree
Of that alone true loyalty
Which, ſacrificing, is not nice
About the terms of ſacrifice,
But offers all, with ſmiles that ſay,
'T were nothing if 't were not for aye !

BOOK II.

JANE.

I.

MRS. GRAHAM TO FREDERICK.

MRS. GRAHAM TO FREDERICK.

I WEEP for your great grief, dear Boy,
  And not lefs for your lofty joy.
You wanted her, my Son, for wife,
With the fierce need of life in life!
That nobler paffion of an hour
Was rather prophecy than power;
And nature, from fuch ftrefs unbent,
Recurs to deep difcouragement.
Truft not fuch peace yet; eafy breath,
In hot difeafes, argues death;
And tafteleffnefs within the mouth
Worfe fever fhows than heat or drouth.
Wherefore take timely warning, Dear,

Againſt a novel danger near.
Beware leſt that " ill Voice " once more
Should plead, not vainly as before.
Wed not one woman, O my Son,
Becauſe you love another one !
Oft, with a diſappointed man,
The firſt who cares to win him can ;
For, after love's heroic ſtrain,
Which tired the heart and brought no
        gain,
He feels conſoled, relieved, and eaſed
To meet with her who can be pleaſed
To proffer kindneſs, and compute
His acquieſcence for purſuit ;
Who troubles not his lonely mood ;
Aſks naught for love but gratitude ;
And, as it were, will let him weep
Himſelf within her arms to ſleep.
Ah, deſperate folly !   (Though, we know,
Who wed through love wed moſtly ſo.)

Before all elfe, when wed you do,
See that the woman equals you,
Nor rufh, from having loved too high,
Into a worfe humility.
Whofe Child, whofe *Coufin* are you? Wait
Until this blaft fhall well abate!
Though love may feem to have wreck'd
      your life,
Look to the falvage; take no wife
Who to your ftooping feels fhe owes
Her name; fuch debts make bofom-foes.
  A poor eftate's a foolifh plea
For marrying to a bafe degree.
A gentlewoman's twice as cheap,
As well as pleafanter, to keep.
Nor think grown women can be train'd,
Or, if they could, that much were gain'd;
For never was a man's heart caught
By graces he himfelf had taught.
And fancy not 't is in the might

Of man to do without delight;
For fhould you in her nothing find
To exhilarate the higher mind,
Your foul will clog its ufelefs wings
With wickednefs of lawful things,
And vampire pleafure fwift deftroy
Even the memory of joy.
So let no man, in defperate mood,
Wed a dull girl becaufe fhe's good.
All virtues in his wife foon dim,
Except the power of pleafing him,
Which may fmall virtue be, or none!

I know, my juft and tender Son,
To whom the dangerous grace is given
That fcorns a good which is not heaven;
My Child, who ufed to fit and figh
Under the bright, ideal fky,
And pafs, to fpare the farmer's wheat,
The poppy and the meadow-fweet!
He would not let his wife's heart ache

For what was mainly his miftake;
But, having err'd fo, all his force
Would fix upon the hard right courfe.

   I fee you with a vulgar wife!
Or one abforb'd in *future* life,
And in this tranfitory place
Contented with the *means* of grace;
Uncultured, fay, yet good and true,
And therefore inward fair, and, through
The veils which inward beauty fwathe,
All lovely to the eye of faith!
Ah, that's foon fagged; faith falls away,
Without the ceremonial ftay
Of outward lovelinefs and awe.
The weightier matters of the law
She pays; mere mint and cumin not;
And, in the road that fhe was taught,
She treads, and takes for granted ftill
Nature's immedicable ill;
So never wears within her eyes

A falfe report of paradife,
Nor ever modulates her mirth
With vain compaffion of the earth,
Which made a certain happier face
Affecting, and a gayer grace
With pathos delicately edged'!
Yet, though fhe be not privileged
To unlock for you your heart's delight,
(Her keys being gold, but not the right,)
On lower levels fhe may do!
Her joy is more in loving you
Than being loved, and fhe commands
All tendernefs fhe underftands.
It is but when you proffer more,
The yoke weighs heavy and chafes fore.
It's weary work enforcing love
On one who has enough thereof,
And honour on the lowlihead
Of ignorance! Befides, you dread,
In Leah's arms, to meet the eyes

Of Rachel ſomewhere in the ſkies,
And both return, alike relieved,
To life leſs loftily conceived.
Alas, alas !
          Then wait the mood
In which a woman may be woo'd
Whoſe thoughts and habits are too high
For honour to be flattery ;
And ſuch would ſurely not allow
The ſuit that you could proffer now.
Her equal yoke would ſit with eaſe ;
It might, with wearing, even pleaſe,
(Not with a better word to move
The indignant loyalty of love !)
She would not mope when you were
      gay,
For want of knowing aught to ſay ;
Nor vex you with unhandſome waſte
Of thoughts ill-timed and words ill-
      placed ;

7

Nor hold fmall things for duties fmall,
(This brands ill-breeding moſt of all,)
But, gilding uſes with delight,
And comprehending nature right,
Would mend or veil each weaker part
With ſome ſweet ſupplement of art.
Nor would ſhe bring you up a brood
Of ſtrangers bound to you by blood,
Boys of a meaner moral race,
Girls with their mother's evil grace,
But not her right to ſometimes find
Her critic paſt his judgment kind;
Nor, unaccuſtom'd to reſpect,
Which men, where 't is not claim'd,
   neglect,
Confirm you ſelfiſh and moroſe,
And ſlowly by contagion groſs;
But, glad and able to receive
The honour you would long to give,
Would haſten on to juſtify

Your hope of her, however high,
Whilſt you would happily incur
Compulſion to keep up with her.

    Paſt price is ſuch a woman, yet
Not rare, nor hard for *you* to get ;
And ſuch, in marrying, yields ſo much
It could not leſs than greatly touch
The heart of him who call'd her Bride,
With tenderneſs, and manly pride,
And ſoft, protective, fond regard,
And thoughts to make no duty hard.

    Your love was wild, (but none the leſs
Praiſe be to love, whoſe wild exceſs
Reveals the honour and the height
Of life, and the ſupreme delight
In ſtore for all but him who lies
Content in mediocrities !)
To wed with one leſs loved may be
Part of divine expediency.
Many men cannot love ; more yet

Cannot love fuch as they can get,
Who ftill fhould marry, and do, and find
Comfort of heart and peace of mind
More than when love-fick fpirits dull
The force of manhood mafterful,
Which woman's foftneffes require,
And women ever moft admire.

II.

FREDERICK TO HIS MOTHER.

FREDERICK TO HIS MOTHER.

YOUR letter, Mother, bears the date
    Of fix months back, and comes too
      late.
My Love, paft all conceiving loft,
A change feem'd good, at any coft,
From lonely, ftupid, filent grief,
Vain, objectlefs, beyond relief,
And like a fea-fog fettled denfe
On fancy, feeling, thought, and fenfe.
I grew fo idle, fo defpifed
Myfelf, my powers, by her unprized;
Honouring my poft, but nothing more;
And lying, when I lived on fhore,

So late of mornings; fharp tears ftream'd
For fuch flight caufe,— if only gleam'd,
Remotely, forrowfully bright,
On clouded eves at fea, the light
Of Englifh headlands in the fun,—
That foon I deem'd 't were better done
To lay this poor, complaining wraith
Of unreciprocated faith;
And fo, with heart ftill bleeding quick,
But ftrengthen'd by the comfort fick
Of knowing that *fhe* could not care,
I turn'd my back on my defpair;
And told our chaplain's daughter, Jane,—
A dear, good Girl, who faw my pain,
And fpoke as if fhe pitied me,—
How glad and thankful I fhould be
If fome kind woman, not above
Myfelf in rank, would give her love
To one that knew not how to woo.
Whereat fhe, without more ado,

Bluſh'd, ſpoke of love return'd, and cloſed
With what I meant to have propoſed.
  And, truſt me, Mother, I and Jane
Suit one another well. My gain
Is very great in this good wife,
To whom I'm bound, for natural life,
By hearty faith, yet croſſing not
My faith towards — I know not what !
As to the ether is the air,
Is her good to Honoria's fair ;
One place is full of both, yet each
Lies quite beyond the other's reach
And recognition. Star and ſtar,
Rays croſſing, cloſer rivals are,
Sequeſter'd in their ſeparate ſpheres.
And now, except ſome caſual tears,
The old grief lives not. If you ſay,
Am I contented ? Yea and nay !
For what's baſe but content to grow
With leſs good than the beſt we know ?

But think me not from fenfe withdrawn
By paffion for a hope that's gone,
So far as to forget how much
A woman is, as merely fuch,
To man's affection.   What is beft,
In each, belongs to all the reft ;
And though, in marriage, quite to kifs
And half to love the cuftom is,
'T is fuch difhonour, ruin bare,
The foul's interior defpair,
And life between two troubles toff'd,
To me, who think not with the moft ;
Whatever 't would have been before
My Coufin's time, 't is now fo fore
A treafon to the abiding throne
Of that fweet love which I have known,
I cannot live fo, and I bend
My mind perforce to comprehend
That He who gives command to love
Does not require a thing above

The ſtrength he gives. The higheſt de-
    gree
Of the hardeſt grace, humility;
The ſtep t'wards heaven the lateſt trod,
And that which makes us moſt like God,
And us much more than God behoves,
Is, to be humble in our loves.
Henceforth forever therefore I
Renounce all partiality
Of paſſion. Subject to control
Of that perſpective of the ſoul
Which God himſelf pronounces good,
Confirming claims of neighbourhood,
And giving man, for earthly life,
The cloſeſt neighbour in a wife,
I'll ſerve all. Jane be much more dear
Than others as ſhe's much more near!

    Is one unlovable, and would
We love him, let us do him good!
How eaſy, then, the effect to raiſe

Where naught's amifs but homely ways.
I love her, love her!   Sweet tears come
Of this my felf-will's martyrdom ;
And fweet tears are love's teft, for love
Is naught without the joy thereof.
    Yet, not to lie for God, 't is true
That 't was another joy I knew
When freighted was my heart with fire
Of fond, irrational defire
For fafcinating, female charms,
And hopelefs heaven in two white arms.
" There's nothing half fo fweet in life,"
As the old fong fays ; and I nor wife
Nor Heaven affront, if I profefs,
That care for heaven with me were lefs
But that I'm utterly imbued
With faith of all Earth's good renew'd
In realms where no fhort-coming pains
Expectance, and dear love difdains
Time's treafon, and the gathering drofs,

And lafts forever in the glofs
Of melting.

         All the bright paft feems,
· Now, but a vifion in my dreams,
Which fhows, albeit the dreamer wakes,
The ftandard of right life.   Life aches
To be therewith conform'd ; but, oh !
The world's fo ftolid, dark, and low !
That and the mortal element
Forbid its beautiful intent,
And, like the unborn butterfly,
It feels the wings, and wants the fky.
  But perilous is the lofty mood
Which cannot pull with lowly good !
Right life, for me, is life that wends
By lowly ways to lofty ends.
I well perceive, at length, that hafte
T'wards heaven itfelf is only wafte ·
And thus I dread the impatient fpur
Of aught that fpeaks too plain of Her.

There's little here that ftory tells;
But mufic talks of nothing elfe.
Therefore, when mufic breathes, I fay,
(And bufier urge my tafk,) Away!
Thou art the voice of one I knew,
But what thou fay'ft is not yet true;
Thou art the voice of her I loved,
And I would not be vainly moved.
   Thus love, which did from death fet
      free
All things, now dons death's mockery,
And takes its place with things that are
But little noted. Do not mar
For me your peace! My health is high.
The proud poffeffion of mine eye
Departed, I am much like one
Who had by haughty cuftom grown
To think gilt rooms, and fpacious grounds,
Horfes, and carriages, and hounds,
Fine linen, and an eider bed

As much his need as daily bread,
And honour of men as much or more ;
Till, ftrange misfortune fmiting fore,
His pride all goes to pay his debts,
A lodging anywhere he gets,
And takes his wife and child thereto
Weeping, and other relics few,
Allow'd, by them that feize his pelf,
As precious only to himfelf.
But, foon, kind compenfations, all
Unlook'd for, eafe his cruel fall ;
The fun ftill fhines ; the country green
Has many riches, poorly feen
From blazon'd coaches ; grace at meat
Goes well with thrift in what they eat ;
And there's amends for much bereft
In better thanks for much that's left.
  For Jane, dear Mother, what at firft
You'll fee in her is all the worft.
I'll fay, at once, in outward make,

She is not fair enough to wake
The wifh for fair.   She bears the bell,
However, where no others dwell;
And features fomewhat plainly fet,
And homely manners, leave her yet
The crowning boon and most exprefs
Of Heaven's inventive tendernefs,
A woman.   But I do her wrong,
Letting the world's eyes guide my tongue!
For, fince 't was for my peace, I 've grown
More learned in my tafte, and own
A fort of handfomenefs that pays
No homage to the hourly gaze,
And dwells not on the arch'd brow's
          height
And lids which foftly lodge the light,
Nor in the pure field of the cheek
Flowers, though the foul be ftill to feek;
But fhows as fits that folemn place
Whereof the window is the face:

Blanknefs and leaden outlines mark
What time the Church within is dark;
Yet view it on a Sunday night,
Or fome occafion elfe for light,
And each ungainly line is feen
Some fpecial character to mean
Of Saint or Prophet, and the whole
Blank window is a living fcroll.

 Her knowledge and converfing powers,
You'll find, are. poor. The clock, for
   hours,
Loud clicking on the mantel-fhelf,
Has all the talking to itfelf.
But to and fro her needle runs
Twice, while the clock is ticking once;
And, when a wife is well in reach,
Not filence feparates, but fpeech;
And I, contented, read, or fmoke
And idly think, or idly ftroke
The winking cat, or watch the fire,

In focial peace that does not tire;
Until, at eafeful end of day,
She moves, and puts her work away,
And, faying "How cold 't is," or "How
       warm,"
Or fomething elfe as little harm,
Comes, ufed to finding, kindly prefl'd,
A woman's welcome to my breaft,
With all the great advantage clear
Of none elfe having been fo near.
   But fometimes, (how fhall I deny!)
There falls, with her thus fitting by,
Dejection, and a chilling fhade.
Remember'd pleafures, as they fade,
Salute me, and, in fading, grow,
Like footprints in the thawing fnow.
I feel opprefl'd beyond my force
With foolifh envy and remorfe.
I love this woman, but I might
Have loved fome elfe with more delight;

And ſtrange it ſeems of God that He
Should make a vain capacity.
 Such times of ignorant relapſe,
'T is well ſhe does not talk, perhaps.
The dream, the disſcontent, the doubt,
To ſome injuſtice flaming out,
Were't elſe, might leave us both to moan
A kind tradition overthrown,
And dawning promiſe once more dead
In the pernicious lowlihead
Of not aſpiring to be fair.
And what am I that I ſhould dare
Diſpute with God, who moulds one clay
To honour and ſhame, and wills to pay
With equal wages them that delve
About his vines one hour or twelve !

III.

JANE TO MRS. GRAHAM.

JANE TO MRS. GRAHAM.

DEAR Mother-in-Law, dear Fred
    (you've heard
I've married him) fends love, and word
He hopes you'll come and fee us foon.
Dear Fred will be on leave all June,
And, for a week, or even more,
We fhall be very glad I'm fure.
Dear Fred faid *I* muft write. He thought
It feem'd fo difrefpectful not.
I'm fure that's the *laft* thing I'd be
To dear Fred's relatives. Both he
And I are well, dear Mrs. Graham,
And truft fincerely you're the fame.

The houſe is rather ſmall we've got,
But dear Fred ſays that yours is not
So large by half; ſo you'll not mind.
If you can't leave your Maid behind,
Who, Fred ſays, always goes with you,
I'll manage ſomehow for her too.
You've heard of Uncle John, no doubt.
My choice, when firſt he found it out,
Diſpleaſed him, till he ſaw dear Fred,
Who, you'll be glad, he thinks well-bred,
And an extremely nice young man.
When I told Uncle John our plan
About you, of his own accord
He ſaid, "Well, Jane, you can't afford
To hire a vehicle, my Dear;
So, while your Mother-in-Law is here,
I'll ſend my carriage every day.
The turnpikes won't be much to pay."
That's the kind ſort of man, you know!
I feel quite ſure you'll like him ſo.

He's well aware your family,
Though you're not rich, is very high,
And therefore he will not negled,
Though rich himfelf, all due refped.

I've heard of your dear daughter Grace,
Who died. I hope to fill her place.
You muft not think, now Fred has got
A clofer tie, that you will not
Be loved juft like you ufed to be.
For my part, I am glad to fee
Affedion. When I have but faid
Your name, I've known him turn quite
      red.
If I bewail our nature's taint,
He fays he has feen a faultlefs Saint.
Of courfe that's you. I think there's none
More kind and juft than your dear Son,
Yet, *between us*, Fred's worldly frame
Muft grieve you much, dear Mrs. Graham;
Who are, I'm fure, from all I've heard,

A veffel chofen of the Lord.
But I have hopes of him ; for, oh,
How can we ever furely know
But that the very darkeft place
May be the fcene of faving grace,
Which foftens even hearts of ftone !
Commending you now to the Throne
Of Mercy, I remain in all,
Dear Mrs. Graham, excufe this fcrawl,
In greateft hafte, but ftill the fame,
Your moft affectionate JANE GRAHAM.

IV.

LADY CLITHEROE TO MARY CHURCHILL.

LADY CLITHEROE TO MARY CHURCHILL.

I'VE dreadful news, my Sifter dear!
   Frederick has married, as we hear,
Some awful girl. This fact we get
From Mr. Barton, whom we met
At Abury once. He ufed to know,
At Race and Hunt, Lord Clitheroe,
Who did not keep him up, of course,
And yet he writes, (could tafte be worfe!)
And tells John he had " feen Fred
      Graham,
Commander of the Wolf, — the fame
The Mefs call'd Jofeph, — with his Wife

Under his arm." He lays his life,
"The fellow married her for love,
For there was nothing elfe to move.
H. is her Shibboleth. 'T is faid
Her Mother was a Kitchen-Maid."

    Poor Fred! What *will* Honoria fay?
She thought fo highly of him. Pray
Tell it her gently, for I'm fure
That, in her heart, fhe liked him more
Than all her Coufins. I've no right,
I know you hold, to truft my fight;
But Frederick's ftate could not be hid!
And Felix, coming when he did,
Was lucky; for Honoria, too,
Was almoft gone. How warm fhe grew
On "worldlinefs," when once I faid
I fancied that in love poor Fred
Had taftes much better than his means!
His hand was worthy of a Queen's,
Said fhe, and actually fhed tears

The night he left us for two years,
And fobb'd, when afk'd the caufe to tell,
That " Frederick look'd fo miferable."
He *did* look very dull, no doubt,
But fuch things girls don't cry about.
  What weathercocks men always prove!
You're quite right not to fall in love.
I never did, and, truth to tell,
I don't think it refpectable.
The man can't underftand it, too!
He likes to be in love with you,
But fcarce knows how, if you love him,
Poor fellow! When it's woman's whim
To ferve her hufband night and day,
The kind foul lets her have her way.
So, if you wed, as foon you fhould,
Be felfifh for your hufband's good!
Happy the men who relegate
Their pleafures, vanities, and ftate
To *us.* Their nature feems to be

To enjoy themſelves by deputy,
For, ſeeking their own benefit,
Dear, what a meſs they make of it!
A man will work his bones away,
If but his wife will only play;
He does not mind how much he's teaſed,
So that his plague looks always pleaſed
And never thanks her, while he lives,
For anything, but what he gives!
It's hard to manage men, we hear!
Believe me, nothing's eaſier, Dear.
The moſt important ſtep by far
Is finding what their colours are.
The next is, not to let them know
The reaſon why they love us ſo.
The indolent droop of a blue ſhawl,
Or gray ſilk's fluctuating fall,
Covers the multitude of ſins
In me; *your* huſband, Love, might wince
At azure, and be wild at ſlate,

And yet do well with chocolate.
Of courfe you'd let him fancy he
Adored you for your piety!
   There, now I've faid enough, my Dear
To make you hate me for a year.
You need not write to tell me fo.
Yours fondly, MILDRED CLITHEROE.

9

V.

JANE TO HER MOTHER.

JANE TO HER MOTHER.

DEAR Mother, Frederick's all, and
    more,
A great deal, than you fay, I'm fure;
And, as you write, of courfe I fee
How glad and thankful I fhould be
For fuch a hufband.   Yet, to tell
The truth, I am fo miferable!
There furely muft be fome miftake.
What *could* he fee in me to take
His fancy!   I remember, though,
He never faid he loved me.   No,
I'm no more fit for Frederick's wife
Than Queen of England.   If my life

Could ferve his very flighteft whim,
I'm fure I'd give it up for him
With pleafure ; but what *fhall* I do !
I find that he's fo great and true
That everything feems falfe and wrong
I've done and thought my whole life long;
And fo, though he is often kind,
And never really crofs, my mind
Is all fo dull and dead with fear
That Yes and No, when he is near,
Is much as I can fay.   He's quite
Unlike what moft would call polite,
And yet, when firft I faw him come
To tea in Aunt's fine drawing-room,
He made me feel fo common.   Oh,
How dreadful if he thinks me fo !
It's no ufe trying to behave
To him.   His eye, fo kind and grave,
Sees through and through me !   Could
            not you,

Without his knowing that I knew,
Aſk him to ſcold me now and then?
Mother, it's ſuch a weary ſtrain
The way he has of treating me,
As if 't was ſomething fine to be
A woman; and appearing not
To notice any faults I've got,
But leaving me to mend, or bear
The guilt unblamed. I'm quite aware,
Of courſe, he knows I'm plain, and ſmall,
Stupid, and ignorant, and all
Awkward and mean. As Frederick theſe,
I ſee the beauty which he ſees
When often he looks ſtrange awhile,
And recollects me with a ſmile.
I wiſh he had that fancied Wife,
With me for Maid, now! all my life
To dreſs her out for him, and make
Her beauty lovelier for his ſake.
To have her rate me till I cried;

Then fee her feated by his fide,
And driven off proudly to the Ball;
Then to ftay up for her, whilft all
The fervants were afleep; and hear
At dawn the carriage rolling near,
And let them in; and hear her laugh,
And boaft he faid that none was half
So beautiful, and that the Queen,
Who danced with him the firft, had feen
And noticed her, and afk'd who was
That lady in the golden gauze!
And then to go to bed, and lie
In a fort of heavenly jealoufy,
Until 't was broad day, and I guefs'd
She flept, nor knew how fhe was blefs'd.

    Mother, I look and feel fo ill;
And foon I fhall be uglier ftill,
You know. But I have heard that men
Never think women ugly then.
Pray write and tell me if that's true.

And pardon me for teafing you
About my filly feelings fo.

    Pleafe, Mother, never let him know
A word of what I write. I'd not
Complain, but for the fear I've got
Of going wild, as I've heard tell
Of fome one fhut up in a cell,
With no one elfe to talk to. He,
Finding that he was loved by me
The moft, might think himfelf to blame;
And I fhould almoft die for fhame.

    When I get up, — that's now at feven,
And 't is not light, — my heart's like
        heaven
At times; for I've a foolifh whim
That Fred loves me as I love him,
And, though I'm neither fair nor wife,
Love, fomehow, makes a woman nice.
But daylight makes the glafs reflect
The fact; and then I recollect

That often in the night things feem
Which are not, though we do not dream.
   If being good would ferve — but oh !
The thought's ridiculous, you know.
Why, I myfelf, I never could
See what's in women's being good.
They've nothing in the world to do
But as it's juft their nature to.
Now, when the men, you know, do right,
They have to try with all their might.
They're fo much nobler !   As for us,
We don't deferve the leaft the fufs
They make about us.
              Mother, mind
You muft not think that he's unkind.
Why, I would rather Frederick
Should hate me, beat me with a ftick,
Than ftop at home all day and coo,
As Aunt likes Uncle John to do.
I'm never prouder, after all,

Than when he ftands, fo ftern and tall,
Before the fire.   With bufy lives,
Men can't love like their idle wives!
And, oh, how dull, whilft they were out,
Had women naught to cry about!

VI.

DR. CHURCHILL TO FREDERICK.

DR. CHURCHILL TO FRED-
ERICK.

DEAR Nephew, we have heard your
    news
From ſtrangers! Be aſſured we uſe
Not lightly to relax our love
Where once 't is bound; and I approve
Your reaſons, whatſoe'er they be,
For ſilence. Yield no leſs to me
For ſaying I wiſh, with all my heart,
Your happineſs, and on the part
Of Mary, who is ſtill at home,
Whenever you may chooſe to come
And bring your Wife, you both will find
A welcome couſinly and kind.

As an old man, a relative,
And churchman, I make free to give
My bleffing, burthen'd with the truth
For want of which the fragile youth
Of wedlock fuffers fhocks and fears,
That fwell the heart with needlefs tears.
I'll not fuppofe that rareft chance
Has fall'n which makes a month's ro-
    mance.
Few, if 't were known, wed whom they
    would ;
And this, like all God's laws, is good.
For naught's fo fad the whole world o'er
As much love which has once been more.
    Glorious for warmth and light is love;
But worldly things in the rays thereof
Extend their fhadows, every one
Falfe as the image which the fun
At noon or eve dwarfs or protracts.
A perilous lamp to light men's acts !

By Heaven's kind, impartial plan,
Well wived is he that's truly man,
If but the woman's womanly,
As fure I am your choice muft be.
Luft of the eyes and pride of life
Perhaps fhe's not.   The better wife !
If it be thus, if you have known
(As who has not?) fome heavenly one
Whom the dull background of defpair
Help'd to fhow forth fupremely fair;
If Memory, ftill remorfeful, fhapes
Young Paffion bringing Efchol grapes
To travellers in the Wildernefs,
This truth will make regret the lefs :
Mighty in love as graces are,
God's ordinance is mightier far ;
And he who is but juft and kind
And patient, fhall for guerdon find,
Before long, that the body's bond
Is all elfe utterly beyond

10

In power of love to actualize
The foul's bond which it fignifies,
And even to deck a wife with grace
External in the form and face.
A five years' wife and not yet fair ?
Blame let the man, not Nature, bear !
For as the fun, warming a bank
Where laft year's grafs droops gray and
       dank,
Evokes the violet, bids difclofe
In yellow crowds the frefh primrofe,
And foxglove hang her flufhing head,
So vernal love, where all feems dead,
Makes beauty abound.
            Nor was that naught,
That trance of joy beyond all thought,
The vifion, in one, of womanhood ;
But for all women holding good !
Should marriage fuch a prologue want,
'T were fordid and moft ignorant

Profanity; but, having this,
'T is honour now, and future blifs.
Life, as a child, is put to play
Love's fimple gamut day by day.
If on this humble tafk he dwells,
Not flying off to fomething elfe,
But as the Mafter bids, devotes
To thefe few oft-repeated notes,
His practice, till fuch comes to be
His fubtle, fmooth celerity
That from his eafy hand they are flung
Like bead-rows by a touch unftrung,
The Mafter, after many days,
Beyond hope fpeaks, "Now go thy ways;
And, in thy fafe and finifh'd art,
Take, with the chime of heaven, thy
    part.

VII.

FREDERICK TO HIS MOTHER.

FREDERICK TO HIS MOTHER.

MOTHER, on my returning home
    Laſt night, I went to my wife's
       room,
Who, whiſpering me that our alarms
Were over, put into my arms
Your Grandſon. And I give you joy
Of what, I 'm told, is a fine boy.
Their notion that he 's juſt like me
Is neither faĉt nor flattery !
To you I 'll own the little wight
Fill'd me, unfatherly, with fright,
So grim it gazed, and out of the ſky
There came, minute, remote, the cry,

Piercing, of original pain.
I put the wonder back to Jane,
Who proffer'd, as in kindly course,
Untried amends for strange divorce.
It guess'd at once, by great good luck,
The clever baby, how to suck!
Yet Jane's delight seem'd dash'd, that I,
Of strangers still by nature shy,
Was not familiar quite so soon
With her small friend of many a moon.

But when the new-made Mother smiled,
She seem'd herself a little child,
Dwelling at large beyond the law
By which, till then, I judged and saw,
And that fond glow which she felt stir
For it, suffused my heart for her;
To whom, from the weak babe, and thence
To me, an influent innocence,
Happy, reparative of life,
Came, and she was indeed my wife,

As there lovely with love fhe lay,
Brightly contented all the day
To hug her fleepy little boy
In the reciprocated joy
Of touch, the childifh fenfe of love,
Ever inquifitive to prove
Its ftrange poffeffion, and to know
If the eyes' report be really fo.

She wants his name to be like mine,
But I demur, at twenty-nine,
To being call'd "Old Frederick."
Her father's, Richard, would be "Dick;"
So John has now been fix'd upon,
After her childlefs Uncle John,
Who owns the Grimfley Powder-Mill,
And, perhaps, may put him in his Will.
'T is alfo fettled, fince the mind,
As Jane has heard, may be refined,
In babyhood, by fights that lull
The fenfes with the Beautiful,

That John muſt be refined at once.
No fault of ours if he's a dunce!
She covets, in the ſhower-bath's place,
A marble image of a Grace,
Or, if that coſts too much, a caſt;
But we are both agreed, at laſt,
'T will do to pin a certain ſhawl,
Too gay to wear, againſt the wall,
And let him learn to kick and coo
At lovely ſtripes of red and blue.
And, ſince Nurſe ſays that, now-a-days,
Boys learn, at ſchool, ſuch wicked ways,
Our John's to be brought up at home.
Nor muſt he take to ſea, but ſome
Leſs perilous and reſtleſs life,
Which will not part him from his wife;
The Law might give his talents play!
It's clear he's clever from the way
He looks about, and frowns, and winks,
Which ſhows that he obſerves and thinks.

VIII.

.

JANE TO MRS. GRAHAM.

JANE TO MRS. GRAHAM.

DEAR Mother, — fuch, if you'll al-
  low,
In *love*, not *law*, I'll call you now, —
I hope you're well.   I write to fay
Frederick has got, befides his pay,
A good appointment in the Docks ;
Alfo to thank you for the frocks
And fhoes for baby.   I, D. v.,
Shall wean him foon.   Fred goes to fea
No more.   I *am* fo glad ; becaufe,
Though kinder hufband never was,
He feems ftill kinder to become
The more he ftays with me at home.

When we've been parted, I fee plain
He's dull till he gets ufed again
To marriage.   Do not tell him, though;
I would not have him know I know,
For all the world.

             How good of you
Not, as I've heard fome mothers do,
To hate his wife!   I try to mind
All your advice; but fometimes find
I do not well know how.   I thought
To take it about drefs; fo bought
A gay new bonnet, gown, and fhawl;
But Frederick was not pleafed at all;
For, though he fmiled, and faid, " How
        fmart! "
I feel, you know, what's in his heart.
But I fhall learn!   I fancied long
That care in drefs was very wrong,
Till Frederick, in his ftartling way
When I began to blame, one day,

The Admiral's wife, becaufe we hear
She fpends two hours, or fomething near,
In dreffing, took her part, and faid
How all things deck themfelves that wed;
How birds and plants grow fine to pleafe
Each other in their marriages;
And how (which certainly is true —
It never ftruck me — did it you?)
Drefs was, at firft, Heaven's ordinance,
And has much Scripture countenance.
For Eliezer, we are told,
Adorn'd with jewels and with gold
Rebecca.   In the Pfalms, again,
How the King's Daughter dreff'd!   And,
        then,
The Good Wife in the Proverbs, fhe
Made herfelf clothes of tapeftry,
Purple, and filk: and there's much more
I had not thought about before!
It's ftrange how well Fred underftands

A Book I don't fee in his hands
At all, except at Church.

            Do you know,
Since Baby came, he loves me fo!
I'm really ufeful, now, to Fred;
And none could do fo well inftead.
It's nice to fancy, if I died,
He'd mifs me from the Darling's fide!
Alfo, there's fomething now, you fee,
On which we talk, and quite agree;
On which, without pride too, I can
Hope I am wifer than a man.
I fhould be happy now, if quite
Convinced that Frederick was right
About religion; but he's odd,
And very feldom fpeaks of God;
And, though I truft his prayers are faid,
Becaufe he goes fo late to bed,
I doubt his calling.   Glad to find
A text adapted to his mind,

I ſhow'd him Thirty-three and four
Of Chapter ſeven, firſt of Cor.,
Which ſeems to allow, in Man and Wife,
A little worldlineſs of life.
He ſmiled, and ſaid that he knew all
Such things as that without Saint Paul!
And once he ſaid, when I with pain
Had got him juſt to read Romaine,
" Men's creeds ſhould not their hopes
       condemn.
Who wait for heaven to come to them
Are little like to go to heaven,
If logic's not the devil's leaven! " ·
I cried at ſuch a wicked joke,
And he, ſurpriſed, went out to ſmoke.
   But to judge him is not for me,
Who ſin myſelf ſo dreadfully
As half to doubt if I ſhould care
To go to heaven, and he not there.
He *muſt* be right; and I dare ſay ·

I foon fhall underftand his way.
To other things, once ftrange, I 've grown
Accuftom'd, nay, to like.   I own
'T was long before I grew well ufed
To fit, while Frederick read or mufed
For hours, and fcarcely fpoke.   When he,
For all that, held the door to me,
Picked up my handkerchief, and rofe
To fet my chair, with other fhows
Of honour, fuch as men, 't is true,
To fweethearts and fine ladies do,
It almoft feem'd an unkind jeft ;
But now I like thefe ways the beft.
They fomehow help to make me good ;
And I don't mind his quiet mood.
If Frederick *does* feem dull awhile,
There 's Baby.   You fhould fee him fmile!
I 'm pretty and nice to him, fweet Pet,
And he will learn no better yet ;
And when he 's big and wife, you know,

There 'll be new babes to think me fo,
Indeed, now little Johnny makes
A bufier time of it, and takes
Our thoughts off one another more,
I 'm happy as need be, I 'm fure!

BOOK III.

RACHEL.

I.

JANE TO MRS. GRAHAM.

JANE TO MRS. GRAHAM.

DEAR Mrs. Graham, the fever's paſt,
And we're all well. I, in my laſt,
Forgot to ſay that, while 't was on,
A lady, call'd Honoria Vaughan,
One of Fred's Saliſbury Couſins, came.
Had I, ſhe aſk'd me, heard her name?
'T was that Honoria, no doubt,
Whom Fred would ſometimes talk about
And ſpeak to, when his nights were bad,
And ſo I told her that I had.
She look'd ſo beautiful and kind!
And ſo much like the wife my mind
Was fond of picturing for Fred,

'Thofe wretched years we firft were wed,
Before I gueff'd, or ufe could prove,
The fort of things my hufband loved ;
And how juft living with me was,
In fome ftrange way, the deareft caufe
For liking, and, inftead of charms,
Was being accuftom'd to my arms ;
And even how my getting ill,
And nervous, crofs, and uglier ftill,
And bringing him all kinds of care,
Affected him like growing fair ;
And how, by his brave fingers preff'd,
The blifter, that would burn my breaft
And only make his own to fmart,
Drew the proud flefh from either's heart;
And fo, for all indignities
Of life in health and in difeafe,
His friendlinefs got more and more !

    Of this great joy to make quite fure,
I afk'd once, (when he could not fee,)

Why fuch things made him fond of me?
He kiff'd me and faid, the honour due
To the weaker veffel furely grew
With the veffel's weaknefs!

                I 'll go on,
However, about Mrs. Vaughan.
Vifiting, yefterday, fhe faid,
The Admiral's Wife, fhe learn'd that
     Fred
Was very ill; fhe begg'd to be,
If poffible, of ufe to me.
What could fhe do? Laft year, Fred's
     Aunt
Died, leaving her, who had not a want,
Her fortune. Half was his, fhe thought;
But Fred, fhe knew, would ne'er be
     brought
To take his rights at fecond-hand!
Yet fomething might, fhe hoped, be
     plann'd

With me, which even Frederick,
As favour done to *her*, would like.
What did I think of putting John
To fchool and college ?   Mr. Vaughan,
When John was old enough, could give
Preferment to her relative,
In Government or Church.   I faid
I felt quite fure that deareft Fred
Would be fo thankful.   Would we come,
And make ourfelves, then, quite at home,
Next month, at High-Hurft ?   Change
          of air
Both he and I fhould need, and there
At leifure we could talk, and fix
Our plans, as John was nearly fix.

     It feemed fo rude to think and doubt,
So I faid, Yes.   In going out,
She faid, "How odd of Frederick, Dear,"
(I wifh'd he had been there to hear,)
" To fend no cards, or tell me what

A nice new Coufin I had got!
Was'nt that kind?

        When Fred grew ftrong,
I had, I found, done very wrong.
For the firft time, his voice and eye
Were angry.　But, with folks fo high
As Fred and Mrs. Vaughan and you,
It's hard to guefs' what's right to do!
And he won't teach me.

           Dear Fred wrote,
Dire&ctly, fuch a lovely note,
Which, though it undid all I'd done,
Was, both to me and Mrs. Vaughan,
So kind!　His words, I can't fay why,
Like foldiers' mufic, made me cry.

  Do, Mother, afk dear Fred to go
Without me!　I can't leave, you know,
The babes.　Befides, 't were folly ftark
For *me* to go to High-Hurft Park.
I'm not fo awkward as I was;

But, all confuſed, and juſt becauſe
By chance he call'd me " Love" to-day,
I made ſuch haſte out of his way
I overſet my chair ; whereat
Fred laugh'd, and on the ſpitting cat
The fire-ſcreen tumbled ; ſo I tried
Theſe riſks no more, and ſtood and cried,
And hid for ſhame my burning face,
To hear he liked " that kind of grace."
Fancy if ſuch a thing was done
Where ladies move like Mrs. Vaughan !
But deareſt Fred *ſhould*, once a year,
Juſt get a ſight of his own ſphere.

II.

LADY CLITHEROE TO MARY CHURCHILL.

LADY CLITHEROE TO MARY CHURCHILL.

DEAR Saint, I'm ftill at High-Hurft
  Park.
The houfe is fill'd with folks of mark.
Honoria fuits a good eftate
Much better than I hoped.   How fate
Pets her with happinefs and pride !
And fuch a loving lord, befide !
But, between us, Sweet, everything
Has limits, and to build a wing
To this old houfe, when Courtholm ftands
Empty upon his Berkfhire lands,
And all that Honor might be near

Papa, was buying love *too* dear.
And yet, to fee mild Mrs. Vaughan
Shining on all fhe looks upon,
You'd think that none could ftand more
          high
Than others in her charity;
And to behold her courtly lord
Converfe with her acrofs the board,
'T would feem that part of perfect life
Was not to covet one's own wife.
The hypocrites!
                    Love, there are two
Guefts here, whofe names will ftartle
          you,
Mr. and Mrs. Frederick Graham!
I thought he ftay'd away for fhame.
He and his wife were afk'd, you know,
And would not come, four years ago.
You recollect Mifs Smythe found out
Who fhe had been, and all about

The Chaplain and the Powder-Mill,
And how the fine Aunt tried to inftil
Haut ton, and how, at laft, poor Jane
Had got fo fhy and *gauche* that, when
The Dockyard gentry came to fup,
She always had to be lock'd up ;
And fome one wrote to John and faid
Her mother was a Kitchen-Maid.
Dear Mary, you 'll be charm'd to know
It *muft* be all a fib.   But, oh,
She *is* the oddeft little Pet
On which my eyes were ever fet !
She's fo *outrée* and natural
That, when fhe firft arrived, we all
Wonder'd, as when a robin comes
In through the window to eat crumbs
At breakfaft with us.   She has fenfe,
Humility, and confidence ;
And, fave in dreffing juft a thought
Gayer in colours than fhe ought,

(To-day she looks a cross between
Gypsy and Fairy, red and green,)
All that she does is somehow well.
And yet one never quite can tell
What she *might* do or utter next.
Lord Clitheroe is much perplex'd ;
Her husband, every now and then,
Looks nervous ; all the other men
Are charm'd.   Yet she has neither grace,
Nor one good feature in her face.
Her eyes, indeed, flame in her head,
Like very altar-fires to Fred,
Whose step she follows everywhere,
Like a tame duck, to the despair
Of Colonel Holmes, who does his part
To break her funny little heart.
Honor's enchanted.   'T is her view
That people, if they're good and true,
And treated well, and let alone,
Will kindly take to what's their own,

And always be original,
Like children.   (Honor's juft like all
The reft of us!   But, thinking fo,
It's well fhe miff'd Lord Clitheroe,
Who hates originality,
Though he puts up with it in me!)
   Poor Mrs. Graham has never been
To the Opera!   You fhould have feen
The innocent way fhe told the Earl
She thought Plays finful when a girl,
And now fhe never had a chance!
Frederick's complacent fmile and glance
Towards her, fhow'd me, paft a doubt,
Honoria had been quite cut out.
It's very odd; for Mrs. Graham,
Though   Frederick's   fancy   none   can
            blame,
Seems the *laft* woman you'd have thought
Her lover would have ever fought!
She never reads, I find, nor goes

Anywhere; fo that I fuppofe
She came at all fhe ever knew
By lapping milk, as kittens do.
 Talking of kittens, by the by,
You've much more influence than I
With dear Honoria. Get her, Dear,
To be a little more fevere
With thofe fweet children. They've the
   run
Of all the houfe. When fchool was done,
Maude burft in, while the Earl was there,
With "O Mamma, do be a bear!"
They come on with the fruit, and climb
In people's laps, and all the time
Eat, and we ladies have to rife,
Left Frank fhould die of ftrawberries.
 And there's another thing, my Love,
I wifh you'd fhow you don't approve,
(But perhaps you do!) Though all confefs
Her tact is abfolute in drefs,

She does not get her things fo *good*
As, with her fortune now, fhe fhould.
I feel quite certain, between us,
She cheats her hufband, (fhe did thus
With dear Papa,) and has no end
Of pin-money, full half to fpend
On folks who think themfelves in this
Paid takers of her tolls to Blifs.

    She has her faults, but I muft fay
She's handfomer, in her quiet way,
Than ever! This odd wife of Fred
Adores his old love in his ftead.

III.

JANE TO MRS. GRAHAM.

JANE TO MRS. GRAHAM.

MOTHER, at laſt, we are really come
To High-Hurſt. Johnny ſtays at home.
We ſettled that it muſt be ſo,
For he has been to Aunt's, at Stowe,
And learn'd to leave his h's out ;
And people like the Vaughans, no doubt,
Would think this dreadful.   I, at firſt,
Half fear'd this viſit to the Hurſt.
Fred muſt, I knew, be ſo diſtreſſ'd
By aught in me unlike the reſt
Who come here.   But I find the place
Delightful ; there's ſuch eaſe and grace

And kindnefs, and all feem to be
On fuch a high equality.
They have not got to think, you know,
How far to make the money go.
But Frederick fays it's lefs the expenfe
Of money, than of found good fenfe,
Quicknefs to care what others feel,
And thoughts with nothing to conceal;
Which I'll teach Johnny. Mrs. Vaughan
Was waiting for us on the Lawn,
And kiff'd and call'd me " Coufin." Fred
Neglected his old friends, fhe faid.
He laugh'd, and redden'd up at this.
She was, I think, a flame of his;
But I'm not jealous ! Luncheon done,
I left him, who had juft begun
To talk about the chance of war,
With an old Lady, Lady Carr,—
A Countefs, but I'm more afraid,
A great deal, of the Lady's maid,—

And went with Mrs. Vaughan to fee
The pictures, which appear'd to be
Of forts of horfes, boors, and cows
Call'd Wouvermans, and Cuyps, and Dows.
And, then, fhe took me up, to fhow
Her bedroom, where, long years ago,
A Queen flept. 'T is all tapeftries
Of Cupids, Gods, and Goddeffes ;
And black, carved oak. A curtain'd door
Leads, thence, into her bright boudoir,
Where even her hufband may but come
By favour. He, too, has his room,
Kept facred to his folitude.
Did I not think the plan was good ?
She afk'd me ; but I faid how fmall
Our houfe was, and that, after all,
Though Fred would never fay his prayers
At night, till I was fafe upftairs,
I thought it wrong to be fo fhy
Of being good when I was by.

"Oh, you fhould humour him!" fhe faid,
With her fweet voice and fmile; and led
The way to where the children ate
Their dinner, and Mifs Williams fate.
She's only Nurfery-Governefs,
Yet they confider her no lefs
Than Lord or Lady Carr, or me.
Juft think how happy fhe muft be!
The Ball-Room, with its painted fky,
Where heavy angels feem to fly,
Is a dull place; its fize and gloom
Make them prefer, for drawing-room,
The Library, all done up new
And comfortable, with a view
Of Salifbury Spire between the boughs.
 When fhe had fhown me through the
  houfe,
(I wifh I could have let her know
That fhe herfelf was half the fhow,
She *is* fo handfome and fo kind,)

She had the children down, who had
    dined,
And, taking one in either hand,
Show'd me how all the grounds were
    plann'd.
The lovely garden gently ſlopes
To where a curious bridge of ropes
Croſſes the Avon to the Park.
We reſted by the ſtream, to mark
The brown backs of the hovering trout.
Frank tickled one, and took it out
From under a ſtone. We ſaw his owls,
And awkward Cochin China fowls,
And ſhaggy pony in the croft;
And then he dragg'd us to a loft,
Where pigeons, as he puſh'd the door,
Fann'd clear a breadth of duſty floor,
And ſet us coughing. I confeſs
I trembled for my nice ſilk dreſs.
I cannot think how Mrs. Vaughan

Ventured with that which fhe had on,—
A mere white wrapper, with a few
Plain trimmings of a tranquil blue,
But, oh, fo pretty !   Then the bell
For dinner rang.   I look'd quite well,
("Quite charming" were the words Fred
          faid,)
In the new gown that I've had made
At Salifbury.   In the drawing-room
Was Mr. Vaughan, juft then come home.
I thought him rather cold, but find
That he's at heart extremely kind.
He's Captain of the Yeomanry,
And Magiftrate, and has to fee
About the paupers and the roads ;
And Fred fays he has written odes
On Mrs. Vaughan, to fend her praife,
Like Laura's, down to diftant days.
So fhe deferves !   What caufe there is,
I know not, though, for faying this,

But that fhe looks fo kind and young,
And every word's a little fong.

   I *am* fo proud of Frederick,
He's fo high-bred and lordly-like
With Mrs. Vaughan! He's not quite fo
At home with me; but that, you know,
I can't expect, or wifh. 'T would hurt,
And feem to mock at my defert.
Not but that I'm a duteous wife
To Fred; but in another life,
Where all are fair that have been true,
I hope I fhall be graceful too,
Like Mrs. Vaughan. And, now, Good-
     bye.
That happy thought has made me cry.

13

IV.

HONORIA VAUGHAN TO DR. CHURCHILL.

HONORIA VAUGHAN TO DR. CHURCHILL.

DEAREST Papa, at last we are come,
    The tiresome season over, home!
How honourable it seems to me!
I am sick of town society,
The Opera, and the flatteries
Of cynic, disrespectful eyes!
    Frederick is here.   Tell Mrs. Fife;
Who adored him.   He has brought his
        wife.
She *is* so nice; but Felix goes
Next Sunday with her to the Close,
And you will judge her.   She the first

Has made me jealous, though the Hurſt
Is lit ſo oft with lovelineſs,
And, when in town, where I was leſs
Conſtrain'd in choice, I always aſk'd
The prettieſt. Felix really baſk'd
Like Puſs in fire-ſhine, when the room
Was all aflame with female bloom ;
And, ſince I praiſed and did not pout,
His little, lawleſs loves went out
With the laſt brocade. 'T is not the
            ſame,
I find, with Mrs. Frederick Graham !
I muſt not have her ſtopping here
More than a fortnight once a year.
My huſband ſays he never ſaw
Such proof of what he holds for law,
That beauty is love which can be ſeen.
Whatever he by this may mean,
Were it not fearful if he fell
In love with her on principle !

Felix has fpoken only twice :
Once on Savoy, and once on this
Shameful Reform Bill ; and on each
He made a moft fuccefsful fpeech ;
And both times I, of courfe, was there
And heard him cheer'd.   But, (how un-
     fair !)
Whenever, wifhing to explain
His meaning, he got up again,
They call'd out "Order," and " Oh, oh !"
He abufed the Newfpapers, and fo
The "Times" left out the cries of "Hear."
The very Oppofition cheer
Dear Felix ; and at what he faid
The Arch-Radical turn'd white and red.
I faw him with my opera-glafs.
Yet they allow'd the law to pafs
The fecond reading.   Should this cheat
Succeed next fpring, we lofe our feat !
Nor fhall I grieve.   The wifeft fay

There's near at hand an evil day;
And, though, if Felix chofe to ftir,
I am fure he might be Minifter,
I tell him, they ferve England moft
Who keep, at whatfoever coft,
Their honour; and, when beft and firft
Have flung their ftrength to laft and worft,
And ruling means, from hour to hour
Cajoling thofe who have the power,
A gentleman fhould ftay at home,
And let his rulers fometimes come
And blufh at his high privacy.
Felix, I know, agrees with me,
Although he calls me, "Fierce white cat!"
And fays, 't is not yet come to that.

    Yefterday, he and I fell out;
Can you believe it? 'T was about
The coft at which he fays I dreff'd
Laft feafon. *I* came off the beft;
And you, Papa, by both ftand talk'd

Inftead, as you fhall learn : I afk'd,
Would he, at one houfe, think it nice
To fee me in the fame drefs twice ?
Of courfe he kiff'd me, and faid, " No ! "
And then I proved, *he* made me go
To Lady Lidderdale's three fetes
And both her dances ! *Magiftrates*
Ought to know better than to try
A charge difmiff'd ; and he and I
Had talk'd this over once before !
Forgiv'n, he vow'd to offend no more.
But, oh, he actually fays
You caution'd him againft my ways :
We both are fhock'd Papa could be
So cruel and unfatherly !

V.

FREDERICK TO HIS MOTHER.

COULD any, whilſt there's any woe,
    Be wholly bleſt, the Vaughans
    were ſo!
Each is, and is aware of it,
The other's endleſs benefit;
But, though their daily ways reveal
The depth of private joy they feel,
'T is not their bearing each to each
That does abroad their ſecret preach,
But ſuch a lovely good-intent
To all within their government
And friendſhip, as, 't is well diſcern'd,
Each of the other muſt have learn'd;

For no mere faith of neighbourhood
Ever begot fo fair a mood.
　　Honoria, made more dove-like mild
With added loves of lord and child,
Is elfe unalter'd.　Years, that wrong
The reft, touch not her beauty, young
With youth that feems her natal
　　　　clime,
And no way relative to time.
All in her prefence generous grow,
As in the funfhine flowers blow ;
As colours, each fuperb to fight,
When all combined are only light,
Her many noble virtues mifs
Proud virtue's blazon, and are blifs ;
The ftandards of the depth are furl'd ;
The　powers　and　pleafures · of　the
　　　　world
Pay tribute ; and her days are all
So high, pure, fweet, and practical,

She almoſt ſeems to have, at home,
What's promiſed of the life to come.

    And fair, in faĉt, ſhould be the few
God dowers with nothing elſe to do ;
And liberal of their light, and free
To ſhow themſelves, that all may ſee !
For alms let poor men poorly give
The meat whereby men's bodies live ;
But they of wealth are ſtewards wiſe
Whoſe graces are their charities.

    The funny charm about this home
Makes all to ſhine who thither come.
My own dear Jane has caught its grace,
And does an honour to the place.
Acroſs the lawn I lately walk'd
Alone, and watch'd where moved and
          talk'd,
Gentle and goddeſs-like of air,
Honoria and ſome ſtranger fair.
I choſe a path away from theſe ;

When one of the two Goddeſſes,
With my wife's voice, but ſofter, ſaid,
" Will you not walk with us, dear
        Fred ? "
    She moves, indeed, the modeſt peer
Of all the proudeſt ladies here.
'T is wonderful ſhe ſhould not be
Put out by ſuch fine company.
We daily dine with men who ſtand
Among the leaders of the land,
And women beautiful and wiſe,
With England's greatneſs in their eyes.
To high, traditional good-ſenſe,
And knowledge vaſt without pretence,
And human truth exactly hit
By quiet and concluſive wit,
Liſtens my little, homely dove,
Miſtakes the points, and laughs for love.
You ſhould have ſeen the vain delight,
After we went upſtairs laſt night,

With which fhe ftood and comb'd her
      hair,
And call'd me much the wittieft there !
  With recklefs loyalty, dear Wife,
She lays herfelf about my life !
The joy I might have had of yore
I have not ; for 't is now no more,
With me, the lyric time of youth,
And glad fenfation of the truth ;
Yet, beyond hope or purpofe bleft,
In my rafh choice, let be confefs'd
The tenderer Providence that rules
The fates of children and of fools !
  I kifs'd the kind, warm neck that flept,
And from her fide this morning ftepp'd,
To bathe my brain from drowfy night
In the fharp air and golden light.
The dew, like froft, was on the pane.
The year begins, though fair, to wane.
There is a fragrance in its breath

14

Which is not of the flowers, but death,
And green above the ground appear
The lilies of another year.
I wandered forth, and took my path
Among the bloomlefs aftermath ;
And heard the fteadfaft robin fing,
As if his own warm heart were fpring,
And watch'd him feed where, on the yew,
Hung fugar'd drops of crimfon dew ;
And then return'd, by walls of peach
And pear-trees bending to my reach,
And rofe-buds with the rofes gone,
To bright-laid breakfaft.   Mrs. Vaughan
Was there, none with her.   I confefs
I love her rather more than lefs !
But fhe alone was loved of old ;
Now love is twain, nay, manifold ;
For, fomehow, he whofe daily life
Adjufts itfelf to one true wife,
Grows to a nuptial, near degree

With all that's fair and womanly.
Therefore, as more than friends, we met
Without conftraint, without regret ;
The wedded yoke that each had donn'd
Seeming a fanction, not a bond.

VI.

MRS. GRAHAM TO FREDERICK.

MRS. GRAHAM TO FREDERICK.

A MAN'S taſkmaſters are enough !
    Add not yourſelf to the hoſt
      thereof.
This did you ever from the firſt,
As now, in venturing to the Hurſt.
You won, my child, from weak ſurpriſe,
A vigour to be doubly wiſe.
In wedlock : with ſucceſs, then, ceaſe,
Nor riſk the triumph and the peace.
'T is not pure faith that hazards even
The adulterous hope of change in heaven.
    Your love lacks joy, your letter ſays.
Yes ; love requires the focal ſpace

Of recollection, or of hope,
Ere it can meafure its own fcope.
Too foon, too foon, comes Death to
    fhow
We love more deeply than we know !
The rain, that fell upon the height
Too gently to be call'd delight,
Within the dark vale reappears,
As a wild cataract of tears ;
And love in life fhould try to fee
Sometimes what love in death would be !
(Eafier to love, we fo fhould find,
It is, than to be juft and kind !)
    She's cold.   Put to the coffin-lid.
What diftance for another did,
That death has done for her ! The good,
Once gazed upon with heedlefs mood,
Now fills with tears the famifh'd eye,
And turns all elfe to vanity.
'T is fad to fee, with death between,

The good we have paſſ'd, and have not
     feen !
How ſtrong appear the words of all !
The looks of thoſe that live appall.
They are the ghoſts, and check the breath;
There's no reality but death,
And hunger for ſome ſignal given
That we ſhall have our own in heaven !
But this the God of love lets be
A horrible uncertainty.

    How great her ſmalleſt virtue ſeems,
How ſmall her greateſt fault ! Ill dreams
Were thoſe that foil'd with loftier grace
The homely kindneſs of her face.
'T was here ſhe fat and work'd, and there
She comb'd and kiſſ'd the children's hair;
Or, with one baby at her breaſt,
Another taught, or huſh'd to reſt.
Praiſe does the heart no more refuſe
To the divinity of uſe.

Her humbleſt good is hence moſt high
In the heavens of fond memory;
And love ſays Amen to the word,
A prudent wife is from the Lord.
Her worſt gown's kept, ('t is now the beſt,
And that in which ſhe ofteneſt dreſſ'd,)
For memory's ſake more precious grown
Than ſhe herſelf was for her own.
Poor wife! fooliſh it ſeem'd to fly
To ſobs inſtead of dignity,
When ſhe was hurt. Now, more than all,
Heart-rending and angelical
That ignorance of what to do,
Bewilder'd ſtill by wrong from you.
(For what man ever yet had grace
Ne'er to abuſe his power and place?)
    No magic of her voice or ſmile
Raiſed in a trice a fairy iſle.
But fondneſs for her underwent
An unregarded increment.

Like that which lifts, through centuries,
The coral reef within the ſeas,
Till, lo! the land where was the wave.
Alas! 't is everywhere her grave.

VII.

FREDERICK TO HIS MOTHER.

FREDERICK TO HIS MOTHER.

A T Jane's defire, left High-Hurft
Park
Should make our cottage cold and dark,
After three weeks we came away
To fpend at home our Wedding-Day.
Twelve wedding-days gone by, and none
Yet kept, to keep them all in one,
She and myfelf, (with John and Grace
On donkeys,) vifited the place
I firft drew breath in, Knatchley Wood.
Bearing the bafket, ftuff'd with food,
Milk, loaves, hard eggs, and marmalade,
I halted where the wandering glade

Divides the thicket.   There I knew,
It feem'd, the very drops of dew
Below the unalter'd eglantine.
Nothing had changed fince I was nine!
   In the green defert, down to eat
We fat, our ruftic grace at meat
Good appetite, through that long climb
Hungry two hours before the time.
And there Jane took her ftitching out,
And John for birds' nefts look'd about,
And Grace and Baby, in between
The warm blades of the breathing green,
Dodged grafshoppers ; and I no lefs,
In confcientious idlenefs,
Enjoy'd myfelf, under the noon
Stretch'd, and the founds and fights of June
Receiving, with a drowfy charm,
Through muffled ear and folded arm.
   And then, as if I fweetly dream'd,
I half remember'd how it feem'd

When I, too, was a little child
About the wild wood roving wild.
Pure breezes from the far-off height
Melted the blindnꜯs from my ſight,
Until, with rapture, grief, and awe,
I ſaw again as then I ſaw.
As then I ſaw, I ſaw again
The harveſt wagon in the lane,
With high-hung tokens of its pride
Left in the elms on either ſide ;
The daiſies coming out at dawn
In conſtellations on the lawn ;
The glory of the daffodil ;
The three black windmills on the hill,
Whoſe magic arms, flung wildly by,
Sent magic ſhadows paſt the rye.
Within the leafy coppice, lo,
More wealth than miſers' dreams could
      ſhow,
The blackbird's warm and woolly brood,

15

Five golden beaks agape for food ;
The Gypfies, all the fummer feen
Native as poppies to the Green ;
The winter, with its frofts and thaws
And opulence of hips and haws ;
The lovely marvel of the fnow ;
The Tamar, with its altering fhow
Of gay fhips failing up and down,
Among the fields and by the Town.
And, dearer far than anything,
Came back the fongs you ufed to fing.
(Ah, might you fing fuch fongs again,
And I, your child, but hear as then,
With confcious profit of the gulf
Flown over from my prefent felf !)
And, as to men's retreating eyes,
Beyond high mountains higher rife,
Still farther back there fhone to me
The dazzling dufk of infancy.
Thither I look'd, as, fick of night,

The Alpine ſhepherd looks to the height,
And does not ſee the day, 't is true,
But ſees the roſy tops that do.
   Meantime Jane ſtitch'd, and fann'd
     the flies
From my repoſe, with huſh'd replies
To Grace, and ſmiles when Baby fell.
Her countenance love viſible
Appear'd, love audible her voice.
Why in the paſt alone rejoice,
Whilſt here was wealth before me caſt
Which, as you ſay, if 't were but paſt
Were then moſt precious ! Queſtion vain
When aſk'd again and yet again,
Year after year ; yet now, for no
Cauſe, but that heaven's bright winds
    will blow
Not at our beck, but as they liſt,
It brought that diſtant, golden miſt
To grace the hour, firing the deep

Of spirit and the drowsy keep
Of joy, till, spreading uncontain'd,
The holy power of seeing gain'd
The outward eye, this owning even,
That where there's love and truth there's
      heaven.

   Debtor to few, far-separate hours
Like this, that truths for me are powers,
(Ah, happy hours, 't is something yet
Not to forget that I forget!)
I know their worth, and this, the chief,
I count not vain because 't was brief.

   And now a cloud, bright, huge, and
      calm,
Rose, doubtful if for bale or balm;
O'ertoppling crags, portentous towers
Appear'd at beck of viewless powers
Along a rifted mountain range.
Untraceable and swift in change,
Those glittering peaks, disrupted, spread

To folemn bulks, feen overhead ;
The funfhine quench'd, from one dark
     form
Fumed the appalling light of ftorm.
Straight to the zenith, black with bale,
The Gypfies' fmoke rofe deadly pale ;
And one wide night of hopelefs hue
Hid from the heart the recent blue.
And foon, with thunder crackling loud,
A flafh within the formlefs cloud
Show'd vague recefs, projection dim,
Lone failing rack, and fhadowy rim.

    We ftood fafe group'd beneath a fhed.
Grace hid behind Jane's gown for dread,
Who told her, fondling with her hair,
" The naughty thunder, God took care
It fhould not hurt good little girls."
At this Grace re-arranged her curls ;
But John, difputing, feem'd to me
Too much for Jane's theology,

Who bade him watch the tempeft. Now
A blaft made all the woodland bow;
Againft the whirl of leaves and duft
Kine dropp'd their heads; the tortured
     guft
Jagg'd and convulfed the afcending fmoke
To mockery of the lightning's ftroke.
The blood prick'd, and a blinding flafh
And clofe, co-inftantaneous crafh
Humbled the foul, and the rain all round
Refilient dimm'd the whiftling ground,
Nor flagg'd in force from firft to laft,
Till, fudden as it came, 't was paft,
Leaving a trouble in the copfe
Of brawling birds and tinkling drops.
    Change beyond hope ! Far thunder
      faint
Mutter'd its vaft and vain complaint,
And gaps and fractures fringed with light
Show'd the fweet fkies, with fquadrons
     bright

Of cloudlets glittering calm and fair
Through gulfs of calm and glittering air.
　With this adventure, we return'd.
The roads the feet no longer burn'd.
A wholefome fmell of rainy earth
Refrefh'd our fpirits, tired of mirth.
The donkey-boy drew friendly near
My wife, and, touch'd by the kind cheer
Her countenance fhow'd, or footh'd per-
　　　chance
By the foft evening's fad advance,
As we were, ftroked the flanks and head
Of the afs, and, fomewhat thick-voiced,
　　　faid,
" To 'ave to wop the donkeys fo
'Ardens the 'art, but they won't go
Without ! " My wife, by this impreff'd,
As men judge poets by their beft,
When now we reach'd the welcome door,
Gave him his hire, and fixpence more.

VIII.

JANE TO MRS. GRAHAM.

JANE TO MRS. GRAHAM.

DEAR Mother, I juft write to fay
    We've paff'd a moft delightful day,
As, no doubt, you have heard from Fred.
(Once, you may recollect, you faid,
True friendfhip neither doubts nor doats,
And does not read each other's notes;
And fo we never do!)   I'll mifs,
For Fred's impatient, all but this:
We fpent — the children, he, and I —
Our wedding anniverfary
In the woods, where, while I tried to keep
The flies off, fo that he might fleep,
He actually kiff'd my foot, —

At leaſt, the beautiful French boot,
Your gift,—and, laughing with no cauſe
But pleaſure, ſaid I really was
The very niceſt little wife;
And that he prized me more than life.
When Fred once ſays a thing, you know,
You feel ſo ſure it muſt be ſo,
It's almoſt dreadful!   Then on love,
And marriage, and the world above,
We talk'd; for, though we ſeldom name
Religion, both now think the ſame.
O Mother, what a bar's removed
To loving and to being loved!
For no agreement really is
In anything when none's in this.
Why, once, if dear, dear Frederick preſſ'd
His wife againſt his hearty breaſt,
The interior difference ſeem'd to tear
My own, until I could not bear
The trouble.   Oh! that dreadful ſtrife,

It ſhow'd indeed that faith is life.
Fred never felt this.   If he did,
I'm ſure it could not have been hid ;
For wives, I need not ſay to you,
Can feel juſt what their huſbands do,
Without a word or look.   But then
It is not ſo, you know, with men.

   And now I'll tell you how he talk'd,
While in the Wood we ſat or walk'd.
He told me that "The Sadducees
Inquired not of true marriages
When they provoked that dark reply,
Which now coſts love ſo many a ſigh.
In vain would Chriſt have taught ſuch
      clods
That Cæſar's things are alſo God's ! "
I can't quite think that happy thought,
It ſeems ſo novel, does it not ?
Fred only means to ſay, you know,
It *may*, for aught we are told, be ſo.

He thinks that joy is never higher
Than when love worſhips its deſire
Far off.   His words were : "After all,
Hope's mere reverſal may befall
The partners of His glories who
Daily is crucified anew :
Splendid privations, martyrdoms
To which no weak remiſſion comes,
Perpetual paſſion for the good
Of them that feel no gratitude,
Far circlings, as of planets' fires,
Round never to be reach'd deſires,
Whatever rapturouſly ſighs
That life is love, love ſacrifice."
And then, as if he ſpoke aloud
To ſome one looking from a cloud,
" All I am ſure of heaven is this,
Howe'er the mode, I ſhall not miſs
One true delight which I have known.
Not on the changeful earth alone

Shall loyalty remain unmoved
T'wards everything I ever loved.
So Heaven's voice calls, like Rachel's voice
To Jacob in the field, 'Rejoice!
Serve on fome feven more fordid years,
Too fhort for wearinefs or tears;
Serve on; then, O Beloved, well-tried,
Take me forever for thy bride!'"

    You fee, though Frederick fometimes
        fhocks
One's old ideas, he's orthodox.
Was it not kind to talk to me
So really confidentially?
    Soon filent, as before, he lay,
But I felt giddy all the day,
And now my head aches; fo farewell!
    Poftfcript. — I've one thing more to
        tell:
Fred's teaching Johnny algebra!
The rogue already treats mamma

As if he thought her, in his mind,
Rather filly, but very kind.
Is not that nice ?   It's fo like Fred !
Good-bye ! for I'm to go to bed,
Becaufe I'm tired, or ought to be.
That's Frederick's way of late.   You fee
He really loves me after all.
He's growing quite tyrannical !

THE END.

☞ Any Books in this list will be sent free of postage, on receipt of price.

BOSTON, 135 WASHINGTON STREET,
DECEMBER, 1860.

A LIST OF BOOKS

PUBLISHED BY

TICKNOR AND FIELDS.

Sir Walter Scott.

ILLUSTRATED HOUSEHOLD EDITION OF THE WAVER-
LEY NOVELS. 50 volumes. In portable size, 16mo. form. Now
Complete. Price 75 cents a volume.

The paper is of fine quality; the stereotype plates are not old
ones repaired, the type having been cast expressly for this edition. The Novels are illustrated with capital steel plates en-
graved in the best manner, after drawings and paintings by the
most eminent artists, among whom are Birket Foster, Darley,
Billings, Landseer, Harvey, and Faed. This Edition contains
all the latest notes and corrections of the author, a Glossary and
Index; and some curious additions, especially in "Guy Man-
nering" and the "Bride of Lammermoor;" being the fullest
edition of the Novels ever published. *The notes are at the foot
of the page,*—a great convenience to the reader.

Any of the following Novels sold separate.

WAVERLEY, 2 vols.	ST. RONAN'S WELL, 2 vols.
GUY MANNERING, 2 vols.	REDGAUNTLET, 2 vols.
THE ANTIQUARY, 2 vols.	THE BETROTHED, } 2 vols.
ROB ROY, 2 vols.	THE HIGHLAND WIDOW, }
OLD MORTALITY, 2 vols.	THE TALISMAN,
BLACK DWARF, } 2 vols.	TWO DROVERS,
LEGEND OF MONTROSE, }	MY AUNT MARGARET'S MIRROR, } 2 vols.
HEART OF MID LOTHIAN, 2 vols.	THE TAPESTRIED CHAMBER, }
BRIDE OF LAMMERMOOR, 2 vols.	THE LAIRD'S JOCK. }
IVANHOE, 2 vols.	WOODSTOCK, 2 vols.
THE MONASTERY, 2 vols.	THE FAIR MAID OF PERTH, 2 vols.
THE ABBOT, 2 vols.	ANNE OF GEIERSTEIN, 2 vols.
KENILWORTH, 2 vols.	COUNT ROBERT OF PARIS, 2 vols.
THE PIRATE, 2 vols.	THE SURGEON'S DAUGHTER, }
THE FORTUNES OF NIGEL, 2 vols.	CASTLE DANGEROUS, } 2 vols.
PEVERIL OF THE PEAK, 2 vols.	INDEX AND GLOSSARY. }
QUENTIN DURWARD, 2 vols.	

TALES OF A GRANDFATHER. *In Press.*

LIFE. By J. G. Lockhart. *In Press.*

Thomas De Quincey.

CONFESSIONS OF AN ENGLISH OPIUM-EATER, AND SUS-
PIRIA DE PROFUNDIS. With Portrait. 75 cents.

BIOGRAPHICAL ESSAYS. 75 cents.

MISCELLANEOUS ESSAYS. 75 cents.

THE CÆSARS. 75 cents.

LITERARY REMINISCENCES. 2 vols. $1.50.

NARRATIVE AND MISCELLANEOUS PAPERS. 2 vols. $1.50.

ESSAYS ON THE POETS, &c. 1 vol. 16mo. 75 cents.

HISTORICAL AND CRITICAL ESSAYS. 2 vols. $1.50.

AUTOBIOGRAPHIC SKETCHES. 1 vol. 75 cents.

ESSAYS ON PHILOSOPHICAL WRITERS, &c. 2 vols. 16mo.
$1.50.

LETTERS TO A YOUNG MAN, AND OTHER PAPERS. 1 vol.
75 cents.

THEOLOGICAL ESSAYS AND OTHER PAPERS. 2 vols
$1.50.

THE NOTE BOOK. 1 vol. 75 cents.

MEMORIALS AND OTHER PAPERS. 2 vols. 16mo. $1.50.

THE AVENGER AND OTHER PAPERS. 1 vol. 75 cents.

LOGIC OF POLITICAL ECONOMY, AND OTHER PAPERS.
1 vol. 75 cents.

Thomas Hood.

MEMORIALS. Edited by his Children. 2 vols. $1.75.

Alfred Tennyson.

POETICAL WORKS. With Portrait. 2 vols. Cloth. $2.00.

POCKET EDITION OF POEMS COMPLETE. 75 cents.

THE PRINCESS. Cloth. 50 cents.

IN MEMORIAM. Cloth. 75 cents.

MAUD, AND OTHER POEMS. Cloth. 50 cents.

IDYLLS OF THE KING. A new volume. Cloth. 75 cents.

Charles Dickens.

[ENGLISH EDITION.]

THE COMPLETE WORKS OF CHARLES DICKENS. Fine Library Edition. Published simultaneously in London and Boston. English print, fine cloth binding, 22 vols. 12mo. $27.50.

Henry W. Longfellow.

POETICAL WORKS. In two volumes. 16mo. Boards. $2.00.
POCKET EDITION OF POETICAL WORKS. In two volumes. $1.75.
POCKET EDITION OF PROSE WORKS COMPLETE. In two volumes. $1.75.
THE SONG OF HIAWATHA. $1.00.
EVANGELINE: A Tale of Acadia. 75 cents.
THE GOLDEN LEGEND. A Poem. $1.00.
HYPERION. A Romance. $1.00.
OUTRE-MER. A Pilgrimage. $1.00.
KAVANAGH. A Tale. 75 cents.
THE COURTSHIP OF MILES STANDISH. 1 vol. 16mo. 75 cents.
Illustrated editions of EVANGELINE. POEMS, HYPERION, THE GOLDEN LEGEND, and MILES STANDISH.

Charles Reade.

PEG WOFFINGTON. A Novel. 75 cents.
CHRISTIE JOHNSTONE. A Novel. 75 cents.
CLOUDS AND SUNSHINE. A Novel. 75 cents.
"NEVER TOO LATE TO MEND." 2 vols. $1.50.
WHITE LIES. A Novel. 1 vol. $1.25.
PROPRIA QUÆ MARIBUS and THE BOX TUNNEL. 25 cts.
THE EIGHTH COMMANDMENT. 75 cents.

James Russell Lowell.

COMPLETE POETICAL WORKS. In Blue and Gold. 2 vols. $1.50.
POETICAL WORKS. 2 vols. 16mo. Cloth. $1.50.
SIR LAUNFAL. New Edition. 25 cents.
A FABLE FOR CRITICS. New Edition. 50 cents.
THE BIGLOW PAPERS. New Edition. 63 cents.
FIRESIDE TRAVELS. *In Press.*

Nathaniel Hawthorne.

TWICE-TOLD TALES. Two volumes. $1.50.
THE SCARLET LETTER. 75 cents.
THE HOUSE OF THE SEVEN GABLES. $1.00.
THE SNOW IMAGE, AND OTHER TALES. 75 cents.
THE BLITHEDALE ROMANCE. 75 cents.
MOSSES FROM AN OLD MANSE. 2 vols. $1.50.
THE MARBLE FAUN. 2 vols. $1.50.
TRUE STORIES. 75 cents.
A WONDER-BOOK FOR GIRLS AND BOYS. 75 cents.
TANGLEWOOD TALES. 88 cents.

Edwin P. Whipple.

ESSAYS AND REVIEWS. 2 vols. $2.00.
LECTURES ON LITERATURE AND LIFE. 63 cents.
WASHINGTON AND THE REVOLUTION. 20 cents.

Charles Kingsley.

TWO YEARS AGO. A New Novel. $1.25.
AMYAS LEIGH. A Novel. $1.25.
GLAUCUS; OR, THE WONDERS OF THE SHORE. 50 cts.
POETICAL WORKS. 75 cents.
THE HEROES; OR, GREEK FAIRY TALES. 75 cents.
ANDROMEDA AND OTHER POEMS. 50 cents.
SIR WALTER RALEIGH AND HIS TIME, &c. $1.25.
NEW MISCELLANIES. 1 vol. $1.00.

Mrs. Howe.

PASSION FLOWERS. 75 cents.
WORDS FOR THE HOUR. 75 cents.
THE WORLD'S OWN. 50 cents.
A TRIP TO CUBA. 1 vol. 16mo. 75 cents.

George S. Hillard.

SIX MONTHS IN ITALY. 1 vol. 16mo. $1.50.
DANGERS AND DUTIES OF THE MERCANTILE PROFES-
SION. 25 cents.
SELECTIONS FROM THE WRITINGS OF WALTER SAVAGE
LANDOR. 1 vol. 16mo. 75 cents.

Oliver Wendell Holmes.

POEMS. With fine Portrait. Cloth. $1.00.
ASTRÆA. Fancy paper. 25 cents.
THE AUTOCRAT OF THE BREAKFAST TABLE. With Il-
lustrations by Hoppin. 16mo. $1.00.
The Same. Large Paper Edition. 8vo. Tinted paper. $3.00.
THE PROFESSOR AT THE BREAKFAST TABLE. 16mo.
$1.00.
The Same. Large Paper Edition. 8vo. Tinted paper. $3.00.
SONGS IN MANY KEYS. A new volume. *In Press.*
CURRENTS AND COUNTER-CURRENTS, AND OTHER MEDI-
CAL ESSAYS. *In Press.*

Ralph Waldo Emerson.

ESSAYS. 1st Series. 1 vol. $1.00.
ESSAYS. 2d Series. 1 vol. $1.00.
MISCELLANIES. 1 vol. $1.00.
REPRESENTATIVE MEN. 1 vol. $1.00.
ENGLISH TRAITS. 1 vol. $1.00.
POEMS. 1 vol. $1.00.
CONDUCT OF LIFE. 1 vol. $1.00. *Nearly ready.*

Goethe.

WILHELM MEISTER. Translated by *Carlyle*. 2 vols. $2.50.
FAUST. Translated by *Hayward*. 75 cents.
FAUST. Translated by *Charles T. Brooks*. $1.00.
CORRESPONDENCE WITH A CHILD. *Bettina*. 1 vol. 12mo.
   $1.25.

Henry Giles.

LECTURES, ESSAYS, &c. 2 vols. $1.50.
DISCOURSES ON LIFE. 75 cents.
ILLUSTRATIONS OF GENIUS. Cloth. $1.00.

John G. Whittier.

POCKET EDITION OF POETICAL WORKS. 2 vols. $1.50.
OLD PORTRAITS AND MODERN SKETCHES. 75 cents.
MARGARET SMITH'S JOURNAL. 75 cents.
SONGS OF LABOR, AND OTHER POEMS. Boards. 50 cts.
THE CHAPEL OF THE HERMITS. Cloth. 50 cents.
LITERARY RECREATIONS, &c. Cloth. $1.00.
THE PANORAMA, AND OTHER POEMS. Cloth. 50 cents.
HOME BALLADS AND POEMS. A new volume. 75 cents.

Capt. Mayne Reid.

THE PLANT HUNTERS. With Plates. 75 cents.
THE DESERT HOME: OR, THE ADVENTURES OF A LOST
   FAMILY IN THE WILDERNESS. With fine Plates. $1.00.
THE BOY HUNTERS. With fine Plates. 75 cents.
THE YOUNG VOYAGEURS: OR, THE BOY HUNTERS IN
   THE NORTH. With Plates. 75 cents.
THE FOREST EXILES. With fine Plates. 75 cents.
THE BUSH BOYS. With fine Plates. 75 cents.
THE YOUNG YAGERS. With fine Plates. 75 cents.
RAN AWAY TO SEA: AN AUTOBIOGRAPHY FOR BOYS.
   With fine Plates. 75 cents.
THE BOY TAR: A VOYAGE IN THE DARK. A New
   Book. With fine Plates. 75 cents.
ODD PEOPLE. With Plates. 75 cents..
The Same. Cheap Edition. With Plates. 50 cents.
THE BOY'S BOOK OF ANIMALS. With Plates. *In Press.*

Rev. F. W. Robertson.

Sermons. First Series. $1.00.
 " Second " $1.00.
 " Third " $1.00.
 " Fourth " $1.00.
Lectures and Addresses on Literary and Social Topics. $1.00.

Mrs. Jameson.

Characteristics of Women. Blue and Gold. 75 cents.
Loves of the Poets. " " 75 cents.
Diary of an Ennuyée. " " 75 cents.
Sketches of Art, &c. " " 75 cents.
Studies and Stories. " " 75 cents.
Italian Painters. " " 75 cents.
Legends of the Madonna. " " 75 cents.
Sisters of Charity. 1 vol. 16mo. 75 cents.

Grace Greenwood.

Greenwood Leaves. 1st and 2d Series. $1.25 each.
Poetical Works. With fine Portrait. 75 cents.
History of my Pets. With six fine Engravings. Scarlet cloth. 50 cents.
Recollections of my Childhood. With six fine Engravings. Scarlet cloth. 50 cents.
Haps and Mishaps of a Tour in Europe. $1.25.
Merrie England. 75 cents.
A Forest Tragedy, and other Tales. $1.00.
Stories and Legends. 75 cents.
Stories from Famous Ballads. Illustrated. 50 cents.
Bonnie Scotland. Illustrated. *Nearly Ready.*

Mrs. Mowatt.

Autobiography of an Actress. $1.25.
Plays. Armand and Fashion. 50 cents.
Mimic Life. 1 vol. $1.25.
The Twin Roses. 1 vol. 75 cents.

Samuel Smiles.

LIFE OF GEORGE STEPHENSON, ENGINEER. $1.00.
SELF HELP; WITH ILLUSTRATIONS OF CHARACTER AND
   CONDUCT. With Portrait. 1 vol. 75 cents.
BRIEF BIOGRAPHIES. With Plates. $1.25.

Miss Cummins.

EL FUREIDIS. By the Author of " The Lamplighter," &c.
   $1.00.

Thomas Hughes.

SCHOOL DAYS AT RUGBY. By *An Old Boy*. 1 vol. 16mo.
   $1.00.
The Same. Illustrated edition. $1.50.
THE SCOURING OF THE WHITE HORSE, OR THE LONG
   VACATION HOLIDAY OF A LONDON CLERK. By *The Author
   of " School Days at Rugby."* 1 vol. 16mo. $1.00.
TOM BROWN AT OXFORD. A Sequel to School Days at
   Rugby. Parts I. to XI. 12 cents each.
The Same. Part First. 1 handsome volume, 400 pages.
   Cloth. $1.00.

François Arago.

BIOGRAPHIES OF DISTINGUISHED SCIENTIFIC MEN.
   16mo. 2 vols. $2.00.

Bayard Taylor.

POEMS OF HOME AND TRAVEL. Cloth. 75 cents.
POEMS OF THE ORIENT. Cloth. 75 cents.
A POET'S JOURNAL. *In Press.*

John Neal.

TRUE WOMANHOOD. A Novel. 1 vol. $1.25.

Hans Christian Andersen.

THE SAND-HILLS OF JUTLAND. 1 vol. 16mo. 75 cents.

R. H. Dana, Jr.

To CUBA AND BACK, a Vacation Voyage, by the Author of
"Two Years before the Mast." 75 cents.

Miscellaneous Works in Poetry and Prose.

[POETRY.]

ALFORD'S (HENRY) POEMS. 1 vol. 16mo. Cloth. $1.00.
ANGEL IN THE HOUSE: THE BETROTHAL. 1 vol. 16mo.
Cloth. 75 cents.
"   "   THE ESPOUSALS. 1 vol. 16mo.
Cloth. 75 cents.
ARNOLD'S (MATTHEW) POEMS. 1 vol. 75 cents.
AYTOUN'S BOTHWELL. A Narrative Poem. 1 vol. 75
cents.
BAILEY'S (P. J.) THE MYSTIC. 1 vol. 16mo. Cloth.
50 cents.
"   "   THE AGE. 1 vol. 16mo. Cloth. 75
cents.
BARRY CORNWALL'S ENGLISH SONGS AND OTHER
POEMS. 1 vol. $1.00.
"   "   DRAMATIC POEMS. 1 vol. $1.00.
BOKER'S PLAYS AND POEMS. 2 vols. 16mo. Cloth.
$2.00.
BROOKS' GERMAN LYRICS. 1 vol. $1.00.
"   FAUST. A new Translation. 1 vol. $1.00.
BROWNING'S (ROBERT) POEMS. 2 vols. $2.00.
"   "   MEN AND WOMEN. 1 vol. $1.00.
CARY'S (ALICE) POEMS. 1 vol. $1.00.
CARYS' (PHŒBE) POEMS AND PARODIES. 1 vol. 75 cts.
FRESH HEARTS THAT FAILED. By the Author of "The
New Priest." 1 vol. 50 cents.
HAYNE'S POEMS. 1 vol. 63 cents.
"   AVOLIO AND OTHER POEMS. 1 vol. 16mo.
Cloth. 75 cents.
HUNT'S (LEIGH) POEMS. 2 vols. Blue and Gold. $1.50.
"   "   RIMINI. 1 vol. 50 cents.
HYMNS OF THE AGES. 1 vol. $1.00.
The Same. A fine edition. 8vo. Bevelled boards. $3.00.
HYMNS OF THE AGES. 2d Series. *In Press.*
JOHNSON'S (ROSA V.) POEMS. 1 vol. $1.00.
KEMBLE'S (MRS.) POEMS. 1 vol. $1.00.

LOCKHART'S (J. G.) SPANISH BALLADS. With Portrait.
1 vol. 75 cents.
LUNT'S (GEO.) LYRIC POEMS. 1 vol. 16mo. Cloth.
63 cents.
"   "   JULIA. 1 vol. 50 cents.
MACKAY'S POEMS. 1 vol. $1.00.
MASSEY'S (GERALD) POEMS. 1 vol. Blue and Gold. 75 cents.
MEMORY AND HOPE. A Collection of Consolatory Pieces.
1 vol. $2.00.
MILNES'S POEMS. 1 vol. 88 cents.
MOTHERWELL'S POEMS. 1 vol. Blue and Gold. 75 cts.
"   MINSTRELSY, ANCIENT AND MODERN.
2 vols. $1.50.
MULOCH'S (MISS) POEMS. (By Author of "John Halifax.") 1 vol. 75 cents.
OWEN MEREDITH'S POEMS. 1 vol. Blue and Gold. 75 cents.
PARSONS'S POEMS. 1 vol. $1.00.
"   DANTE'S INFERNO. Translated. *In Press.*
PERCIVAL'S POEMS. 2 vols. Blue and Gold. $1.75.
QUINCY'S (J. P.) CHARICLES. A Dramatic Poem. 1 vol.
50 cents.
"   "   LYTERIA: A Dramatic Poem. 50 cents.
READ'S (T. BUCHANAN) POEMS. New and complete edition. 2 vols. $2.00.
REJECTED ADDRESSES. By Horace and James Smith.
New edition. 1 vol. 63 cents.
SARGENT'S (EPES) POEMS. 1 vol. 50 cents.
SAXE'S (J. G.) POEMS. With Portrait. 1 vol. 75 cents.
"   "   THE MONEY KING AND OTHER POEMS.
With new Portrait. 1 vol. 75 cents.
SMITH'S (ALEXANDER) LIFE DRAMA. 1 vol. 50 cents.
"   "   CITY POEMS. 1 vol. 63 cents.
STODDARD'S (R. H.) POEMS. 1 vol. 63 cents.
"   "   SONGS OF SUMMER. 1 vol. 75 cts.
SPRAGUE'S (CHARLES) POETICAL AND PROSE WORKS.
With Portrait. 1 vol. 88 cents.
THACKERAY'S BALLADS. 1 vol. 75 cents.
THALATTA. A Book for the Seaside. 1 vol. 75 cents.
TUCKERMAN'S POEMS. 1 vol. 75 cents.
WARRENIANA. 1 vol. 63 cents.

[PROSE.]

ALLSTON'S MONALDI. A Tale. 1 vol. 16mo. Cloth.
75 cents.
ARNOLD'S (DR. THOMAS) LIFE AND CORRESPONDENCE.
Edited by A. P. Stanley. 2 vols. 12mo. Cloth. $2.00.

ARNOLD'S (W. D.) OAKFIELD. A Novel. 1 vol. 16mo.
Cloth. $1.00.

ALMOST A HEROINE. By the Author of " Charles Au-
chester." 1 vol. 16mo. Cloth. $1.00.

ARABIAN DAYS' ENTERTAINMENT. Translated from the
German, by H. P. Curtis. Illustrated. 1 vol. $1.25.

ADDISON'S SIR ROGER DE COVERLEY. From the " Spec-
tator." 1 vol. 16mo. Cloth. 75 cents.

The Same. 1 vol. 16mo. Cloth, gilt edge. $1.25.

ANGEL VOICES; OR, WORDS OF COUNSEL FOR OVER-
COMING THE WORLD. 1 vol. 16mo. Cloth, gilt, 38; gilt
edge, 50; full gilt, 63 cents.

AMERICAN INSTITUTE OF INSTRUCTION. Lectures deliv-
ered before the Institute in 1840–41–42–43–44–45–46–47–48–49–
50–51–52–53–54–55–56–57–58–59. 20 vols. 12mo. Sold in separate volumes, each 50 cents.

BACON'S (DELIA) THE SHAKSPERIAN PROBLEM SOLVED.
With an Introduction by Nathaniel Hawthorne. 1 vol. 8vc.
Cloth. $3.00.

BARTOL'S CHURCH AND CONGREGATION. 1 vol. 16mc.
Cloth. $1.00.

BAILEY'S ESSAYS ON OPINIONS AND TRUTH. 1 vol.
16mo. Cloth. $1.00.

BARRY CORNWALL'S ESSAYS AND TALES IN PROSE.
2 vols. $1.50.

BOSTON BOOK. Being Specimens of Metropolitan Literature. Cloth, $1.25; gilt edge, $1.75; full gilt, $2.00.

BUCKINGHAM'S (J. T.) PERSONAL MEMOIRS. With Portrait. 2 vols. 16mo. Cloth. $1.50.

CHANNING'S (E. T.) LECTURES ON RHETORIC AND ORA-
TORY. 1 vol. 16mo. Cloth. 75 cents.

CHANNING'S (DR. WALTER) PHYSICIAN'S VACATION.
1 vol. 12mo. Cloth. $1.50.

COALE'S (DR. W. E.) HINTS ON HEALTH. 1 vol. 16mo.
Cloth. 63 cents.

COMBE ON THE CONSTITUTION OF MAN. 30th edition.
12mo. Cloth. 75 cents.

CHAPEL LITURGY. Book of Common Prayer, according
to the use of King's Chapel, Boston. 1 vol. 8vo. Sheep, $2.00;
sheep, extra, $2.50; sheep, extra, gilt edge, $3.00; morocco,
$3.50; do. gilt edge, $4.00; do. extra gilt edge, $4.50.

The Same. Cheaper edition. 1 vol. 12mo. Sheep, $1.50.

CROSLAND'S (MRS.) LYDIA: A WOMAN'S BOOK. 1 vol.
75 cents.

　　"　　　"　　ENGLISH TALES AND SKETCHES.
1 vol. $1.00.

CROSLAND'S (MRS.) MEMORABLE WOMEN. Illustrated.
1 vol. $1.00.

DANA'S (R. H.) TO CUBA AND BACK. 1 vol. 16mo.
Cloth. 75 cents.

DUFFERIN'S (LORD) YACHT VOYAGE. 1 vol. 16mo.
Cloth. $1.00.

EL FUREIDIS. By the author of "The Lamplighter."
1 vol. 16mo. Cloth. $1.00.

ERNEST CARROLL; OR, ARTIST-LIFE IN ITALY. 1 vol.
16mo. Cloth. 88 cents.

FREMONT'S LIFE, EXPLORATIONS, AND PUBLIC SER-
VICES. By C. W. Upham. With Illustrations. 1 vol. 16mo.
Cloth. 75 cents.

GASKELL'S (MRS.) RUTH. A Novel. 8vo. Paper. 38 cts.

GUESSES AT TRUTH. By Two Brothers. 1 vol. 12mo.
$1.50.

GREENWOOD'S (F. W. P.) SERMONS OF CONSOLATION.
16mo. Cloth, $1.00; cloth, gilt edge, $1.50;
morocco, plain gilt edge, $2.00; morocco,
extra gilt edge, $2.50.

"   HISTORY OF THE KING'S CHAPEL, BOS-
TON. 12mo. Cloth. 50 cents.

HODSON'S SOLDIER'S LIFE IN INDIA. 1 vol. 16mo. Cloth.
$1.00.

HOWITT'S (WILLIAM) LAND, LABOR, AND GOLD. 2 vols.
$2.00.

"   "   A BOY'S ADVENTURES IN AUSTRA-
LIA. 75 cents.

HOWITT'S (ANNA MARY) AN ART STUDENT IN MUNICH.
$1.25.

"   "   A SCHOOL OF LIFE. A Story.
75 cents.

HUFELAND'S ART OF PROLONGING LIFE. 1 vol. 16mo.
Cloth. 75 cents.

JERROLD'S (DOUGLAS) LIFE. By his Son. 1 vol. 16mo.
Cloth. $1.00.

"   "   WIT. By his Son. 1 vol. 16mo.
Cloth. 75 cents.

JUDSON'S (MRS. E. C.) ALDERBROOK. By Fanny For-
rester. 2 vols. $1.75.

"   "   THE KATHAYAN SLAVE, AND
OTHER PAPERS. 1 vol. 63 cents.

"   "   MY TWO SISTERS: A SKETCH
FROM MEMORY. 50 cents.

KAVANAGH'S (JULIA) SEVEN YEARS. 8vo. Paper. 30
cents.

KINGSLEY'S (HENRY) GEOFFRY HAMLYN. 1 vol. 12mo.
Cloth. $1.25.

KRAPF'S TRAVELS AND RESEARCHES IN EASTERN
AFRICA. 1 vol. 12mo. Cloth. $1.25.

LESLIE'S (C. R.) AUTOBIOGRAPHICAL RECOLLECTIONS.
Edited by Tom Taylor. With Portrait. 1 vol. 12mo. Cloth.
$1.25.

LAKE HOUSE. From the German of Fanny Lewald. 1 vol. 16mo. Cloth. 75 cents.

LOWELL'S (REV. DR. CHARLES) PRACTICAL SERMONS. 1 vol. 12mo. Cloth. $1.25.

" " OCCASIONAL SERMONS. With fine Portrait. 1 vol. 12mo. Cloth. $1.25.

LIGHT ON THE DARK RIVER; OR, MEMOIRS OF MRS. HAMLIN. 1 vol. 16mo. Cloth. $1.00.
The Same. 16mo. Cloth, gilt edge. $1.50.

LONGFELLOW (REV. S.) AND JOHNSON (REV. S.) A book of Hymns for Public and Private Devotion. 6th edition. 63 cents.

LABOR AND LOVE. A Tale of English Life. 1 vol. 16mo. Cloth. 50 cents.

LEE'S (MRS. E. B.) MEMOIR OF THE BUCKMINSTERS. $1.25.

" " FLORENCE, THE PARISH ORPHAN. 50 cents.

" " PARTHENIA. 1 vol. 16mo. $1.00.

LUNT'S (GEORGE) THREE ERAS IN THE HISTORY OF NEW ENGLAND. 1 vol. $1.00.

MADEMOISELLE MORI: A Tale of Modern Rome. 1 vol. 12mo. Cloth. $1.25.

M'CLINTOCK'S NARRATIVE OF THE SEARCH FOR SIR JOHN FRANKLIN. Library edition. With Maps and Illustrations. 1 vol. small 8vo. $1.50.
The Same. Popular Edition. 1 vol. 12mo. 75 cents.

MANN'S (HORACE) THOUGHTS FOR A YOUNG MAN. 1 vol. 25 cents.

" " SERMONS. 1 vol. $1.00. *Just Ready.*

MANN'S (MRS. HORACE) PHYSIOLOGICAL COOKERY-BOOK. 1 vol. 16mo. Cloth. 63 cents.

MELVILLE'S HOLMBY HOUSE. A Novel. 8vo. Paper. 50 cents.

MITFORD'S (MISS) OUR VILLAGE. Illustrated. 2 vols. 16mo. $2.50.

" " ATHERTON, AND OTHER STORIES. 1 vol. 16mo. $1.25.

MORLEY'S LIFE OF PALISSY THE POTTER. 2 vols. 16mo. Cloth. $1.50.

MOUNTFORD'S THORPE. 1 vol. 16mo. Cloth. $1.00.

NORTON'S (C. E.) TRAVEL AND STUDY IN ITALY. 1 vol. 16mo. Cloth. 75 cents.

NEW TESTAMENT. A very handsome edition, fine paper and clear type. 12mo. Sheep binding, plain, $1.00; roan, plain, $1.50; calf, plain, $1.75; calf, gilt edge, $2.00; Turkey morocco, plain, $2.50; do. gilt edge, $3.00.

Otis's (Mrs. H. G.) The Barclays of Boston. 1 vol. Cloth. $1.25.

Parsons's (Theophilus) Life. By his Son. 1 vol. 12mo. Cloth. $1.50.

Prescott's History of the Electric Telegraph. Illustrated. 1 vol. 12mo. Cloth. $1.75.

Poore's (Ben Perley) Louis Philippe. 1 vol. 12mo. Cloth. $1.00.

Phillips's Elementary Treatise on Mineralogy. With numerous additions to the Introduction. By Francis Alger. With numerous Engravings. 1 vol. New edition in press.

Prior's Life of Edmund Burke. 2 vols. 16mo. Cloth. $2.00.

Rab and his Friends. By John Brown, M. D. Illustrated. 15 cents.

Sala's Journey Due North. 1 vol. 16mo. Cloth. $1.00.

Sidney's (Sir Philip) Life. By Mrs. Davis. 1 vol. Cloth. $1.00.

Shelley Memorials. Edited by the Daughter-in-law of the Poet. 1 vol. 16mo. 75 cents.

Sword and Gown. By the Author of "Guy Livingstone." 1 vol. 16mo. Cloth. 75 cents.

Shakspear's (Captain H.) Wild Sports of India. 1 vol. 16mo. Cloth. 75 cents.

Semi-Detached House. A Novel. 1 vol. 16mo. Cloth. 75 cents.

Smith's (William) Thorndale; or, The Conflict of Opinions. 1 vol. 12mo. Cloth. $1.25.

Sumner's (Charles) Orations and Speeches. 2 vols. 16mo. Cloth. $2.50.

St. John's Bayle Village Life in Egypt. 2 vols. 16mo. Cloth. $1.25.

Tyndall's (Professor) Glaciers of the Alps. With Illustrations. 1 vol. Cloth. $1.50.

Tyll Owlglass's Adventures. With Illustrations by Crowquill. 1 vol. Cloth, gilt. $2.50.

The Solitary of Juan Fernandez. By the Author of "Picciola." 1 vol. 16mo. Cloth. 50 cents.

Taylor's (Henry) Notes from Life. 1 vol. 16mo. Cloth. 50 cents.

Trelawny's Recollections of Shelley and Byron. 1 vol. 16mo. Cloth. 75 cents.

Thoreau's Walden: A Life in the Woods. 1 vol. 16mo. Cloth. $1.00.

Warren's (Dr. John C.) Life. By Edward Warren, M. D. 2 vols. 8vo. $3.50.

"   "   The Preservation of Health. 1 vol. 38 cents.

Wallis's (S. T.) Spain and her Institutions. 1 vol. 16mo. Cloth. $1.00.

WORDSWORTH'S (WILLIAM) BIOGRAPHY. By Dr. Christopher Wordsworth. 2 vols. 16mo. Cloth. $2.50.

WENSLEY: A STORY WITHOUT A MORAL. 1 vol. 16mo. Paper. 50 cents.

The Same. Cloth. 75 cents.

WHEATON'S (ROBERT) MEMOIRS. 1 vol. 16mo. Cloth. $1.00.

In Blue and Gold.

LONGFELLOW'S POETICAL WORKS. 2 vols. $1.75.

"   PROSE WORKS. 2 vols. $1.75.

TENNYSON'S POETICAL WORKS. 1 vol. 75 cents.

WHITTIER'S POETICAL WORKS. 2 vols. $1.50.

LEIGH HUNT'S POETICAL WORKS. 2 vols. $1.50.

GERALD MASSEY'S POETICAL WORKS. 1 vol. 75 cents.

MRS. JAMESON'S CHARACTERISTICS OF WOMEN. 75 cts.

"   DIARY OF AN ENNUYEE. 1 vol. 75 cts.

"   LOVES OF THE POETS. 1 vol. 75 cts.

"   SKETCHES OF ART, &c. 1 vol. 75 cts.

"   STUDIES AND STORIES. 1 vol. 75 cts.

"   ITALIAN PAINTERS. 1 vol. 75 cents.

"   LEGENDS OF THE MADONNA. 1 vol. 75 cents.

OWEN MEREDITH'S POEMS. 1 vol. 75 cents.

"   LUCILE: A Poem. 1 vol. 75 cents.

BOWRING'S MATINS AND VESPERS. 1 vol. 75 cents.

LOWELL'S (J. RUSSELL) POETICAL WORKS. 2 vols. $1.50.

PERCIVAL'S POETICAL WORKS. 2 vols. $1.75.

MOTHERWELL'S POEMS. 1 vol. 75 cents.

SYDNEY DOBELL'S POEMS. 1 vol. 75 cents.

WILLIAM ALLINGHAM'S POEMS. 1 vol. 75 cents.

HORACE. Translated by Theodore Martin. 1 vol. 75 cts.

Works lately Published.

FAITHFUL FOREVER. By Coventry Patmore, Author of
"The Angel in the House." . 1 vol. *Just Ready.*

OVER THE CLIFFS: A Novel. By Charlotte Chanter,
(a sister of Rev. Charles Kingsley.) 1 vol. $1.00.

THE RECREATIONS OF A COUNTRY PARSON. 1 vol.
$1.25.

Works in the Press,

IN ADDITION TO THOSE ANNOUNCED IN THE FOREGOING
CATALOGUE.

REMINISCENCES OF SCOTTISH LIFE AND CHARACTER.
By Dean Ramsay. From the Seventh Enlarged Edinburgh
Edition. With an American Preface. 1 vol. 16mo.

POEMS BY REV. WM. CROSWELL, D. D. Edited, with a
Memoir, by Rev. Arthur Cleveland Coxe, D. D. 1 vol.

THE LIFE OF FRANCIS BACON. Founded on Original
Letters and Documents. By Hepworth Dixon. 1 vol. 16mo.

THE LIFE AND CAREER OF MAJOR ANDRE. By Win-
throp Sargent. 1 vol. 12mo.

POEMS. By Rose Terry. 1 vol. 16mo.

THE AUTOBIOGRAPHY OF THE REV. DR. ALEXANDER
CARLYLE. Containing Memorials of the Men and Events of
his Times. Edited by John Hill Burton.

SERMONS PREACHED IN HARVARD CHAPEL. By Rev.
Dr. Walker, late President of Harvard University.

THE COMPLETE WORKS OF WALTER SAVAGE LANDOR.
Library Edition. Revised and Edited by the Author.

BEAUTIES OF DE QUINCEY. Selected from the Writings
of the English Opium-Eater. With fine Portrait. 1 vol. 12mo.

FAVORITE AUTHORS: A Companion Book of Prose and
Poetry. With 26 fine Steel Portraits.

HESPERIA. By the late Richard Henry Wilde. 1 vol.

HEROES OF EUROPE. A capital Boy's Book. With 16
Illustrations.

BONNIE SCOTLAND. By Grace Greenwood. Illustrated.

THE SEVEN LITTLE SISTERS, who live in the Round Ball
that floats in the Air. Illustrated.